THE EXPLORERS

Tides *across the* Sea

Other Books by
Lu Ann Brobst Staheli

Just Like Elizabeth Taylor

Gateway Romance
Temporary Bridesmaid

Small Town U.S.A.
Leona & Me, Helen Marie
A Note Worth Taking

Timeless Romance Anthology
Silver Bells Collection: "A Fezziwig Christmas"

Non-Fiction
Men of Destiny: Abraham Lincoln and the Prophet Joseph Smith
Psychic Madman
When Hearts Conjoin: The True Story of Utah's Conjoined
Twins
One Day at a Time: Teaching Secondary English Language Arts

Books, Books and More Books: A Parent and Teacher's Guide to
Adolescent Literature

THE EXPLORERS

Tides across the Sea

Lu Ann Staheli

Interior Design by Heather Justesen:
www.heatherjustesen.com/typesetting
Edited by Annette Lyon, Heather B. Moore, Michele Paige Homes, Sarah M. Eden and Stephanni Hicken Meyer. Additional editorial input from Sandra Burton, M. Belen Monyano, and Angie Newman Day.

Published by Back Yard Press
ISBN-10:1941145442
ISBN-13:978-1-941145-44-9

To my husband, Mike, who not only introduced me to the idea of a novel about Cortés, but who has also taken me on the greatest adventures of my life.

1

SANTIAGO DE CUBA

Manuela Perez couldn't stop the perspiration pouring across her brow. The azure sky was crisp and clear above the piazza where the sun radiated from the cobblestones, making the day seem hotter. But it was more than the heat making her feel drained. The words coming from the mouth of the boy she hoped to one day marry brought her great worry.

"A *New World*. Just saying the words brings a fire to my belly," Felipe Marco said, reading from one of the many notices posted in the village. Felipe's fists rested on his hips and he pulled his shoulders back, his lean torso enhanced by the muscles bulging from the sleeve above his almond-colored arms. "To travel to a new continent across the Caribbean. This—this would prove to your father that I am a man. Old enough to own a bull and a piece of land, old enough to travel beyond the southern shores of Santiago de Cuba, *and* to marry his daughter."

"Oh, Felipe," Manuela said, sighing. Her tiny frame was almost hidden beneath the orange, yellow, and green ruffles that decorated her skirt and blouse. "What if you never return from this voyage with Cortés? Who would I marry?" She placed her head against the woven fabric of his tunic and touched her creamy palm against his dark curls. The noise of the market swirled around them, but she paid no attention.

A smile played at Felipe's lips as he embraced her. "A child as lovely as you need not worry about marriage." A chuckle rumbled low in his throat. He smoothed his hand across her hair, tucking a loose strand behind her ear.

Manuela pulled herself away, the hair again falling to her cheek. "Child?" Her voice was firm. "I am fifteen, old enough to marry." She tossed her head, turning her back to him for a moment, before she stomped her sandaled foot and kicked Felipe in the shinbone. "I'll show you a child." She pounded against his muscled body with her fists.

"*Cesación! Stop!*" Felipe said, laughing as he fended off her blows.

He hopped on one foot, holding his leg with his right hand. Bumping into a merchant cart filled with oranges, Felipe reached too late to catch the fruit as it tumbled onto the dusty plaza. Three round oranges bounced down the street. A cascade left the cart to follow. Felipe couldn't stop the laughter that escaped his lips.

Nor Manuela hers. Bent over, giggling at the sight of several small children toddling after the bright-colored balls of fruit, she knew she should run to help pick up the damaged wares but could not make herself stop laughing.

2

The merchant was *not* laughing. He was barreling toward her.

"Run!" Felipe called, tossing a few payment coins toward the cart, before he grabbed Manuela's hand and pulled her along with him across the street toward a narrow opening that would lead them away from the fruit merchant, his spilled carts, and the redress they were sure to face if he caught them. Manuela tried to keep an eye toward the merchant's direction as Felipe guided their way through the children and others crowding the streets.

"*Estancia!*" The merchant's voice bellowed as he chased them from the square, his belly heaving with the effort. His steps were slow and the distance between himself and Felipe or Manuela too great for him to snatch hold of either of them. Stopping at the narrow alleyway, he shook his fist at their retreating figures. Manuela saw him glance toward his cart and the children gathering up the last remains of the fruit, which sent him again to the center of the piazza, his hands flying out like he was sending wayward chickens back to their roost. "*Partir!*"

Ensuring their safety, she and Felipe followed a narrow cobblestone path that led farther away from the merchant and into a nearby courtyard. The stones were worn smooth, but dust scuffed around their feet as Felipe pulled Manuela close. "A kick in the shin? Isn't that a little . . . ?"

Manuela interrupted, "Yes, it was childish, but perhaps it is *you* who is too much the child to marry, despite your age." Her tone was playful, the scolding mother who teases her son. "This voyage is a way to escape and play your childish games." Then a wave of sadness settled into her voice as she spoke. "What will I do here without you?"

His voice became soft, nearly buried in the sounds of life around them. "You needn't worry. Captain Cortés hasn't decided I am one who should go." Felipe's brown eyes seemed deep pools, shimmering against the afternoon sun. A look of pain etched his bronze face. "And you know I would rather die than not return to you."

She threw her arms around his neck and nuzzled his throat. For most of his life Felipe had spoken of nothing but joining the great explorer on his next journey. The time had come. A quiver in her voice, Manuela asked, "Do you *really* want to go?" She already knew the answer, but she dared to hope he would change his mind.

Felipe whispered, "Yes."

She drew her eyes to look at him, her fingers still entwined around his neck. She felt a tear against her cheek, but she did not remove her gaze. "Then return home safely to me, Felipe Marco."

"I will." He cleared the sudden huskiness from his voice, pulling her tighter against him. "I will."

Her heart was breaking, but Manuela responded. "And I will wait, no matter how long."

The noise from the busy marketplace rose like waves thundering against the shoreline. How had she missed the rising tide of people who pressed toward the open square? Children, dock workers, merchants and others pushed against the two of them as they stood together, two ships harbored at the same pier. She didn't want to let him go.

After a moment, Felipe stepped away. "But now . . . I must see Cortés. All of my friends want to be chosen as much as I." He touched his finger to the tip of her nose. "The great explorer will never choose me. Never!"

She could tell he was trying to cheer her up. She too would play the game of imagining he would be selected, hoping within her soul that it would not come true. "Talk, all talk. Young boys trying to fill the role of a man." She allowed a smile to cross her lips. "Can you see Eduardo leaving his mother's side for such an adventure?"

The grin on Felipe's face displayed his answer even before he spoke. "No, I can't." He motioned toward the stone edging that surrounded the fountain in the square.

Manuela followed close behind, trying to avoid the people who were now thick around them.

"Only a week ago, he stayed with my family while his parents traveled to visit his father's brother, Señor de Trujillo. Eduardo sniffled and cried all night." Felipe guffawed at the memory. He shook his head a little before continuing. "He claimed it was the dust bothering him, but I know better. His body may say he is almost sixteen, but his emotions do not."

"Infant." Her voice was teasing.

She lifted her skirt from the swirling dust. They had drawn close to the fountain, and she plopped onto the ledge, tucking the brightly-colored fabric beneath her knees. Felipe sat next to her. He surveyed the people rushing past them and raised his hand in greeting to a *niño* younger than he. The boy also waved, but hurried on.

Felipe's tone turned serious. "César is not an infant. Cortés might choose him." Felipe picked up one of her hands and clasped it tightly. A frown creased his brow. "César would be a wise choice."

Manuela knew everyone feared César Caballeria, as did she. He was the strongest of the local youth and a year older than Felipe. She could not control the feelings of fearful weakness that overcame her soul when he was near—a tiny bee hummingbird before the giant iguana. If only César were as harmless as the iguana. Once he had lost a competition against the other boys, and it was Felipe's fault. Accidentally tripped in the last moments of the race, César had fallen, landing sprawled in the dirt like a tree boa knocked from its perch by the great winds of a *huracán*.

Many times since then Manuela had heard Felipe, Eduardo, and their classmate, Miguel, laugh at the memory. If César heard, he raged in response because of the humiliation. Twice he had broken the noses of boys who had gotten near him when he was angry. Maneula worried he was capable of killing one, or all of them.

"Do you think César would be willing to go?" Manuela asked, hopeful. "He is the man of his household now that his papa is dead. Won't his mother need him?" If César were not chosen, staying behind with him could be just as dangerous for her. Already she did not like the bold way César spoke to her, and more than once recently, she had sensed his stare. It made her feel unclean. How bold would he become without Felipe to stand in his way? She chewed the corner of her bottom lip as she considered the possibility.

"She needs him but cannot hold him," Felipe said. "No one can stop César from what he wants to do." He gave a heavy sigh, as though accepting that César would sail with Cortés. His nervous chuckle was cut short when he looked at Manuela.

"Hush. Here he comes now." She stepped behind Felipe, clutching at his garment top as though holding onto a ship's line at the dock.

The stocky lad swaggered in their direction. His broad shoulders lifted as he puffed out his chest and stopped beside them. His soft curly hair seemed out of character for his arrogance. He spoke as though Felipe were not there. "Ah, the lovely Manuela," César said, peering around Felipe's thin form.

"Leave us alone," Felipe said with a sternness Manuela had never heard before.

César spoke as though Felipe had not. "Come out from behind this boy and stand where I can feast upon your beauty." The deep timbre of his voice and the way he stood indicated he did not expect to be ignored.

"No," she said, taking her strength from Felipe.

He reached a protective hand toward Manuela, taking her wrist in his grasp. "What do you want of us?"

"Of you? Nothing." César gave him a dismissive glance, but his eyes softened as he looked at her. "Of Manuela? That is another story. Don't you want something of me, my dear, sweet girl? A kiss, perhaps?"

"No." She turned away, pinching her mouth as though she had tasted a bitter root. "Leave me alone." The stone seat scratched against her calf where she was backed against it, but she would not move away from either Felipe or the fountain. She became aware of the stillness of the courtyard as those near enough to witness paused to listen.

"She wants you to go," said Felipe. "And so do I."

She was so proud of him, the way he stood up to this bully as though unafraid. Perhaps Felipe really had grown up. He was only fifteen, but was it possible he *was* a man, as he wanted her father to believe? Manuela trusted that Felipe would be able to care for her safety, just as she knew he cared about her.

César stood at his full height. His voice deepened with seriousness. He glanced at those standing around the fountain. "What you want matters not to me. I'll leave because I have business with Cortés. But Manuela, you can expect to see me again. Soon I ask for the hand of my bride." An almost playful tone entered his voice. "Perhaps it will be you."

She felt her face drain cold, her stomach roiling at the thought. "Marry you? Never!" She spat into the dirt at her feet.

"Never!" Felipe echoed. "Someday she will marry *me*."

The crowd continued to pass by them, focused on their own destinations.

A deep rumble of laughter escaped from César's lips, breaking the quiet. "We will see. We will see." César nodded curtly to a group of boys standing nearby. They edged closer to the stone edifice of the Santo Domingo church, away from his path as he left the piazza. The rest of the crowd began to talk amongst themselves, continuing their business.

"I hope Cortés takes him," she said, her voice stronger now that she had stood up to her enemy. She let go of Felipe and moved to face him. Noticing his pained expression, she added, "Or perhaps he will take more than one young man. You are not that much different from those two years older."

"He won't," Felipe said, resignation in his voice. "And if César decides he wants to go, Cortés would be a fool not to take him." He dug his great toe into the black soil.

Never had she seen Felipe look so sad. "More so to not choose *you*." She touched her fingertip to his lips.

He reached for her hand, bringing it again to rest between his clasped palms. "Perhaps it would be better if I did not go. I don't want to leave you here unprotected with César. It is not safe."

She placed her other hand over his. "Nonsense. César is too smart to bother me with Papa at home." She hoped her words soothed his concern, although she did not believe them.

Felipe glanced toward the group of boys César had passed. Their voices buzzed as Felipe pulled Manuela with him. The boys appeared to be discussing a parchment posted on the building.

Felipe stopped before the notice, read it, pointed at the intricate markings, then said, "Captain Cortés has a meeting planned this hour for all interested in joining him. This meeting must be where César was headed." He turned to Manuela, excitement in his voice again. "Will you come with me?"

She nodded, the knot in her stomach becoming more

9

pronounced, and they walked toward where Cortés would speak. The group of boys also moved across the courtyard, turning into an alley, and finally emerging at the town's main square. *Does every male in Santiago want to join the voyage?* she wondered.

Manuela had heard her father say King Charles the Fifth, the Holy Roman Emperor, was financing Cortés. The emperor had been present when Christopher Colón returned to Spain to report his conquest to King Ferdinand and Queen Isabella. Now, Charles anticipated the return of his own ships, filled with untold wealth, to the mother country. *Will the men who accompany his envoy also gain riches?* Like with Colón, this new expedition was to travel westward. Manuela did not know where, but she guessed Cortés would take his shipmates as far as necessary in search of gold to bring to his homeland. His king expected it.

The entire grand plaza was filled with anxious applicants. More men laced the surrounding alleyways, likely hoping to glean details from the famous Cortés himself, who was in Santiago, looking for a crew.

"Here's a place," Manuela said, as she pulled Felipe onto a spot near the palace steps. The rough stone stairs were worn, and the arched doorway closed as she leaned against it.

Pointing across her shoulder, Felipe said, "There is César. He will not miss his chance for such an adventure."

She glanced the direction he indicated and saw César, standing as close to the dais as possible. She slipped her hand under Felipe's arm and felt her heart pound.

A lone man stepped onto the raised platform and held up his hand, and the crowd quieted. He stood an average height. An aquiline nose seemed to fill his face—the beak of an *aguila*, the eagle. A thick shock of dark hair made him look like a lad, despite his age and fourteen years of leadership. Although he was now over thirty, the Spaniard was still youthful, especially in the world of explorers.

"I am Hernán Cortés," he said, raising his right hand out to emphasize his announcement. "I am here to select a crew to accompany me on a great voyage. Are there any among you who wish to go?" A deafening roar came from the crowd, and Cortés smiled with apparent pleasure. He raised his arms high, shaking his opened palms in an effort to bring quiet to the crowd. "*Bueno, bueno*," he continued when the response had died. "Let me tell you more."

As the crowd listened, the explorer spoke of great adventure, his plan to bring honor to his country, and the wealth each expedition member could gain. It seemed to Manuela that every man and boy from their city strained to absorb each word he spoke. It would mean much to Felipe if he were chosen, but she feared for his safety. Tales of strange and violent natives in the westward lands lingered from earlier trips by other explorers. *Could Felipe die if he were to go on the journey?*

Felipe leaned forward, as though better proximity would allow him to hear each word more clearly. He clasped his hands together, one over the other, an anxious gesture he'd had since childhood.

This great leader did not impress Manuela. Despite his

black beard, he was no different from a boy. Arrogant. Vain. Boasting only of his adventures with the promise of gold.

"Infant," she said, knowing Felipe could not hear her over the noise. "A child leading children."

2

TENOCHTITLAN, MEXICO

Tia balanced an ornate terra-cotta jug on her head, using both hands and walking carefully to avoid spilling the jug's contents. Carrying water had been her assigned chore for most of her thirteen years. The routine task gave her thoughts a few moments of freedom as a servant in the palace of Moctezuma Xocoyotzin, the absolute ruler of the Mejicas—three years her people.

She stepped onto the path that lead from the aqueduct, past the aviary toward the back of the two-story stone palace the supreme ruler had built—the home Tia no longer wanted. She dreamed of a new land, far away from her spoiled and demanding mistress, Aramonia, wife of the emperor—one of many wives. Passing through the doorway, Tia wound her way toward her mistress's chambers.

"To be free again," Tia said, speaking to no one but herself. She stomped her foot, and a splash of water reminded her she was carrying the jug. "Why did Aramonia choose me?"

"Térahtia!"

At the sound of the angry voice, Tia jumped, spilling more water on her copper skin. She steadied the jug still atop her head with both hands. Aramonia stood in the path, several paces from the entrance to her private quarters. With her mouth drawn tight and her eyes piercing, the queen did not look pleased.

"M'lady," Tia said, as she lowered her head in respect, fearful the queen had heard her previous outburst.

Ten years older than Tia, Aramonia had lived in Teoloyucan when Tia was a toddler. Once or twice Aramonia had cared for the younger girl when her parents were away. *I thought she liked me then.* How she had changed since becoming a wife to Moctezuma.

"Térahtia. The water for my bath."

It was a command, not a question. *When was it otherwise?*

Relief flooded through her. "Sorry, M'lady. I was delayed." She had lost track of time, as she often did when not under Aramonia's strict scrutiny, and she found it better to remain vague in her response—to avoid giving her mistress the full truth.

Hurrying up the steps, Tia slipped past the queen. She carried the jug to the bathing area and poured its cool liquid into the waiting recess. Aramonia followed, stripping off her clothing and stepping into the pool.

"Fetch me a cloth to dry myself with," her mistress said, harshness evident in her tone. "Quick." She lifted the copalxocotl root and rubbed it between her hands then smoothed it along her extended arm.

Tia scurried off, glad to be away a few moments more. She remembered how kind Aramonia had once been, the moments they had played chasing games among the flowers, the sweets the young woman had offered to the small child. How sad it was that the queen's personality had changed when she became Moctezuma's wife. Marriage into the noble class did not suit her well.

Living with the noble class did not suit Tia either. *How I long for escape,* she thought. *All my sadnesses are Moctezuma's fault. My desire for freedom, the ache to see my mother and father, my loneliness—all because Aramonia requested me as her maid.*

Once Tia had heard of a maiden who escaped. It was believed she traveled north to Aztlán, a land far removed from here, and even farther from her southern homeland, Teoloyucan. Aztlán was at the end of the world, as distant away from Moctezuma as anyone could possibly be, farther than a dream.

Moctezuma—the great leader of the Mejicas. "Ha!" Tia laughed aloud as she entered the laundry and gathered an armful of the thick, soft cloths the queen favored.

For years, Moctezuma had been collecting information—stories—about the great white god, Quetzalcóatl. The people believed Moctezuma's interest to be based on a desire to worship this god, but Tia and others of his household knew it was due to fear. The time neared for Quetzalcóatl's foretold return, and Moctezuma was afraid this god would conquer his own holdings. As she carried her load back toward the bath, her thoughts stayed on the country's leader.

15

Rulers should care about their people. They should help them live better lives, not ask them to give their labors only for their leaders.

Moctezuma was arrogant, yet weak and indecisive. The boys in the household whispered gossip about his failures in leadership, never fighting a battle, preferring to spend his hours with his wives and concubines, women collected to prove his power. Tia was glad she had only to deal with *one* of his wives. She rarely saw Moctezuma himself, which pleased her even more.

Returning to the bathing area with the soft cloths, Tia placed them near the edge of the water. "Anything else, Mistress?" she asked, ignoring a woman pouring sweet oils into the bath. The aroma reminded her of the lavender, yellow and white field flowers near Teoloyucan. She missed the fields. She missed the flowers. She missed her mother.

"You are dismissed, Térahtia." Aramonia stretched, then lay her head against a pillow the other servant held in place for her. The queen's morning bath was always longer and more luxurious than the one she took each evening.

"Thank you, M'lady," Tia said, bowing her head as she withdrew.

With no other task at hand, she wandered the lower palace, still thinking of her beloved mother and father who lived far beyond the water. She missed standing amid the towering maize, learning from her parents how to till the land and bring forth food. Tia wanted to return to her mother's side. Wetness coursed her cheeks as she continued to walk the labyrinth below the palace, allowing herself to cry without thought for a destination.

"The prophesy is too ancient to be trusted," a man's voice said as Tia rounded an unfamiliar corner.

She skittered to a halt. *Oh, no. Where am I?* She looked around, disoriented. *Am I in Moctezuma's private suites?*

"The great white god is not due to return until the Year of the Single Reed," another man said.

Where were the guards who should be posted? She had been in the area reserved for the wives and concubines. *How did I come to be here?*

"Next year." The voice was Moctezuma's.

I must escape before he sees me. A glance told her she had a long way to go before she could escape the main corridor. The next cross-entrance was far toward the end of the hall. If she ran, her sandals would make too much noise against the cut stone floor. She would be discovered, and that would guarantee her being among those sacrificed to the gods.

Tia turned. Moctezuma stood directly in front of her, not twenty yards away. His *tilmantli,* a flowing white robe, dropped from his right shoulder to the polished floor. She was grateful the supreme ruler of Tenochtitlan looked away from her. Although his three advisors faced her, their gestures indicated they were trying desperately to convince their lord of something. She hoped they did not see her as she searched for the nearest path of escape. The coarse flax garment she wore blended into the stone as she pressed her back to its cold surface, creeping her way toward the far end of the passage.

A fourth man spoke. "You have nothing to worry about, our master. The Year of the Single Reed has come and passed before in the endless circle of time, with no visit from the Great White god."

"Enough!" the emperor shouted. "Mark my words, Quetzalcóatl will come, and when he does, each of *you* will serve as a sacrifice in the temple."

"Yes, M'Lord," one of the men muttered.

Tia darted into an unseen and welcomed alcove just as Moctezuma swung his cloak and stepped in the direction from which she had come. His companions followed behind, still arguing, trying to catch up with their revered leader.

She stood alone again.

Quetzalcóatl? Everyone knows the great white god is nothing but a myth—everyone except you, Moctezuma. She whispered, "There is no such thing as a white man."

Tia surveyed the hallway from her hiding spot, decided on a direction, and scurried toward what she hoped were her own chambers through the underground labyrinth which made up the secret passageways of the palace.

"A white god, indeed. Fool!"

3

In the two days since Cortés invited men and boys to apply for a position with his crew, Felipe spent his time in whatever tasks he could to keep his mind occupied. He helped his mother and tended his bull. This morning he had talked with his father about working during the harvest. Felipe wanted to buy land for the home he intended to build for Manuela, and today he planned to survey the possibilities.

Then his friend Eduardo flew past him, shouting, "Cortés posted the list! Come on!"

With Eduardo's words his thoughts of the future vanished. The two boys charged toward the town square. Males of all ages joined the race, hoping to find their names on the list. Felipe prayed he could hide his disappointment if his name did not appear.

Pushing his way through the teeming crowd, he panted from the exertion under the Cuban sun; beads of sweat dotted his brow. *What if my name is not on the list?* His heart pounded with anticipation. *César will likely be chosen. But . . .*

"There, see there. At the bottom of the list of men," one of the youth in the already gathered group yelled. "He's is taking two *los jóvenes* with him after all."

Two? Felipe allowed a tiny bit of hope to rise in his breast. He strained to hear the conversations coming from the front of the crowd where the parchment was posted.

"Read the names," another man said.

Silence fell except for sounds of "Shhh." Felipe held his breath. *Will it be me?* The same question was certainly in the minds of most of the assembly. He felt the dampness under his sleeves and tried to steady his knees from swaying, locked into position as they were.

"The first name—César Fernandes Caballeria!"

Dead silence at first then a collective sigh of resignation. The boys mumbled to each other. "I knew it would be him."

The heavy weight of Felipe's heart fell to his stomach. He had expected César would be chosen, but the truth disturbed him all the same.

"What is the next name?" someone shouted. The crowd again quieted.

"The second name is . . ." the boy shouted then paused, increasing the tension in the horde. "Miguel Mauricio Hernandez!" shouted the reader.

The blood rushing in Felpe's head muffled the noise around him. He concentrated on not retching, hoping he didn't pass out in the process.

The silence hung for a second before Miguel let out a

whoop of joy. Immediately, several boys gathered around him in congratulations. Others quietly moved away, slipping into the streets toward their homes. A few stayed to check the list themselves, perhaps reading the names of the men who would also leave.

Felipe placed his hands on his knees and doubled over, allowing deep breaths to charge in and out of his lungs.

"I never would have thought of Miguel," said Eduardo. "Would you?"

Felipe stood for a moment, realizing his friend did not seem to be affected by the announcement, assuming he did not care, although he had said he wanted to be chosen. Had Eduardo applied to go with Cortés, or was he afraid to leave his mother?

"Would you have guessed Miguel?" Eduardo asked, trying again for a response.

Straightening his body, Felipe shook his head, realizing for the first time that, although they were the same age, Eduardo looked much younger than he did. Perhaps his friend really was a child, one who would not be of help to a man like Cortés. "No, I would not have believed he would take Miguel." *Although I had hoped he would take me.* "But, none of us knew he would choose two. Miguel is a good choice. His quietness will be a needed balance to César's arrogance."

"Arrogance is not a strong enough word. Did you notice he did not even come to read the posting?" Eduardo held his hands wide at the side of his head, as though trying to show a skull that was too big. "He holds too high an opinion of himself." His laughter pealed above the noise in the square.

Felipe sighed. "And I suppose well he should. He is the most qualified. Did you ever doubt he would be chosen?"

"No," Eduardo admitted, "but I did hope." The sheepish grin and rosy blush that spread across his face said otherwise.

"As did we all." Felipe tried to smile, but his real feelings showed as he dug his heel deep into the sandy soil. His brow furrowed in thought, as he chewed on his lower lip. "I wonder if we know any of the men on the list."

"Let's see." The dissipating crowd made it possible for the two of them to draw close and scan the entire list. "There are many names I recognize. Jesus Ricardo Peña, Frederico Lopez, and Herberto's father, Bautista Guzman." Eduardo ran his finger down the list. "It will be odd to have so many men gone."

"And for more than a year." *In which I will marry Manuela before César returns.* Staying in Cuba might play out to be the better course after all. A well of satisfaction rose in his breast.

"Felipe!" Manuela cried as she ran across the plaza.

He turned toward the sound of her voice, holding his arms out in her direction. Her dark hair floated behind her, like the colored panels of her skirt in the breeze. She plowed into him and threw her arms around his neck, hugging him tightly. His love for her washed over him like the tides of the ocean on a warm summer day.

"My darling," Felipe said. "You got your wish. I will remain here in Cuba with you. César was so certain of his choice he didn't even come to read the list for himself."

"I know," she said breathlessly. Her voice choked as she continued. "That is what–I came–to tell you. César is at my house as we speak. He came to ask my father about my– dowry."

Eduardo drew in a sharp gasp of surprise.

"Why would he ask about . . . ?" Felipe's eyes narrowed. "No! César told us he would soon ask for a bride, but I thought he was baiting me; I didn't think–"

She pulled away, great tears forming in her eyes. "I didn't either. He knows I hate him."

"And he hates me," Felipe said. *All the more reason to take away that which I most love.* A churning of thoughts rushed toward him. He had to confront César. He glanced toward the direction of her home. Would César still be there?

"What shall we do?" Manuela sobbed. "I won't marry him." She held a lace cloth to her eyes to dab the tears.

"I know what I must do," Felipe said. "I will kill him." He caressed the edge of the lace for a moment, the moisture of her tears embedded in the fabric. Dropping the fabric, he gave a single nod of his head as he began to run.

"Stop!" she cried. "There must be another way."

Manuela took a step toward Felipe's retreating figure, but Eduardo clutched her arm to hold her back. Her cries were unsuccessful as Felipe dashed away, toward her house, and César. Trying to free herself from Eduardo's grip, she demanded, "Let me go." When he didn't, she spat at him in anger.

"Manuela, you must not. It will make him less of a man." Eduardo's tone was firm.

She quit pulling, relaxing the strain of the fabric as he continued to grasp her sleeve. Drawing in a deep breath, she let the air escape through her parted lips. When she no longer resembled the angry bull she felt like, she spoke. "You are right. To prove he is a man is important. It is the reason my father would not listen when Felipe asked for my betrothal. It is the reason he wanted to be chosen by Cortés, to prove to my father he is prepared to care for a wife. He must confront César."

"I will wait to hear from you, Felipe," she called after him.

4

Tia stood patiently behind her mistress in the palace courtyard, listening to Aramonia's conversation with the queen's younger brother, Iccauhtli, the slave trader. Although he usually traveled alone, this time Iccauhtli had brought a new slave into the palace, Doña Marina Malinche from Teoloyucan. Tia longed for someone to talk with—someone who understood what it was like to live outside the city walls. All of the other slaves hailed from Tenochtitlan—or at least the ones she knew. Could this young woman become a friend?

"She is more than an ordinary slave," Iccauhtli said, his words directed toward his sister. "After her mother remarried and bore a son, they no longer wanted the girl who reminded them of a father years dead, so she sold her to me. Her father was a nobleman in the southeast province of Coatzacoalcos."

Used to serving the queen, Tia remained silent, head

bowed as she considered Doña Malinche's history. Daughter
of a nobleman. No longer wanted by a mother who had
given birth to her. How had she been able to bear the loss?

The rich aroma of rain lilies tickled Tia's nose, but she
kept herself from either sneezing or rubbing the offending
spot. She wished to do nothing that would cause her to miss
any detail about the visiting woman.

"Why is she so valuable that you have not yet given her
to trade?" Aramonia asked, her tone sounding eager to know
more.

"She is intelligent. As the child of a nobleman, she
learned many dialects through her travels. She is a woman at
nineteen and could be an asset to me in the business trade
someday."

"Oh," Aramonia said, disappointment evident in her
tone.

Tia had hoped the queen would be anxious to keep
Malinche for yet another of her personal slaves. The idea
brought a beat of hope into her breast. But she knew
Malinche would not be staying long. Her value as an
interpreter and noble parentage almost assured it.

Three years ago, when Iccauhtli had brought Tia herself
to the palace as a slave—an honorable occupation—her
parents had been well-rewarded with several sheep for
sending their daughter into full-time service to the queen.
Flattered at first, Tia loved the beauty of the palace and the
adventure of travel, meeting new people, and learning many
things, especially about different lands. She had begun to
understand new customs and even a few words of the odd

languages and dialects palace visitors spoke. *There is much I could learn from Malinche, especially if she were my friend. Someone I could trust.*

As though she suddenly realized Tia was there, Aramonia turned, startled. "What are you doing, listening to my private conversations? Be gone with you." She moved her hand, an indication Tia was to leave.

Dipping her head once and keeping her eyes down, Tia backed away from the queen. "Yes, M'lady." Wishing she could hear more about Malinche, yet glad for the time to finish her chores, she hurried off to the daily washing, her thoughts occupied by what she already knew about the new slave girl.

Even though Malinche would not stay long, Tia yearned to meet the maiden from her homeland. Malinche did not have assigned household duties, but Moctezuma and Aramonia kept her busy, nonetheless. A few of the other slaves had praised Malinche and talked about how knowledgeable she was. Tia wanted to hear the stories for herself before Malinche and Iccauhtli left, as she knew they would soon be doing.

When it was almost time for the midday break, and Tia's stomach felt empty—the meager respite she had eaten at dawn long past—she entered the dining area, a plain wooden table laden with food dominate in the center of the room. A large group of girls gathered around someone she did not recognize at first. Then she realized the dark beauty must be Malinche.

The special slave sat near the hearth, her feet tucked neatly beneath the embroidered cotton cloth of her floor-length skirt. A golden belt cinched her tiny waist. Strings of beads and gold hung around her bare neck, and her upper arms were banded with wide bracelets. A pale-colored ribbon held her ebony hair away from her face. She balanced a dish of food on her lap while the crowd pressed around her.

Tia looked at her own plain tunic, touched the hair that hung straight down across her shoulders. Would Malinche even be interested in talking to a girl like herself?

"Where do you come from? What of your parents? How long have you been a slave? How do you know so many languages?" Questions from the others flew almost faster than Malinche could answer them. Everyone seemed to be interested in hearing from this young woman, just as Tia was.

"Iccauhtli knew my childhood history from Teoloyucan. When the arrangements for my sale were completed, I left my homeland for the final time." Her voice was deep and rich.

Tia placed some cooked dog meat and sweet potatoes on a saucer then joined the others kneeling near Malinche, who nibbled on a fried corn cake between questions. She listened, sorry that she had missed even a part of the conversation, trying to assemble the threads.

"That is why I am here," Malinche said. "My story is not so much different than any of yours, except perhaps my experience with languages. It is an honor for me to serve in the house of Moctezuma, as it is for each of you."

28

"It is not such an honor," mumbled Rebekha. Younger than Tia, this girl had not yet learned to keep her feelings within her heart, a skill that Tia herself had yet to master.

"Oh, but you are wrong, child," Malinche said as she touched Rebekha's hand. "No matter the circumstances, it is always an honor to serve one's master, especially if he is the supreme ruler."

Tia knew Malinche was wrong. Moctezuma was a difficult man who changed his mind often. She had heard stories from other members of the household regarding punishments received from him when they had carried out his wishes, only to discover they were no longer his wishes. The women murmured about Malinche's comment, and Tia knew they, too, doubted it was an honor to be a servant to one so unpredictable as he.

Jeroni, one of the cooks, turned to the young woman to ask, "Malinche, will you be serving with us?"

"Iccauhtli plans for us to be here several weeks, so I will be assigned tasks," Malinche said. "Most likely I will serve the queen."

Is there a chance Malinche will work with Aramonia? Tia hoped so. *Being a slave might not be so bad if I had memories to keep my heart and mind of her company,* she decided, and Malinche's travels would become her own memories.

"I hear there is one among you who is from my homeland," Malinche said, scanning their faces. "I would like to meet her and share a message from her mother and father. Where is the girl called Térahtia?"

Tia choked on a bite of meat she was swallowing. A

message from my parents? The others turned to look at her with curiosity and envy. She blushed at the unexpected attention then cleared her throat before trying to speak. "I . . . I am Térahtia," she said. "But I am called Tia by my friends."

"Then I hope I may call you Tia," Malinche said, a radiant smile gracing her lips. "Where might we go to talk in private, about your family?"

"I know just the place," Tia said as she rose to clear her dish. Although flustered, she moved across the room, motioning for the young woman to follow.

The other slaves returned to their conversations before the two girls left the room, obviously discussing the things Malinche had told them while they finished their own meals.

She led the way outside and sat with Malinche on the stone ledge of the well. Beneath the blooming wisteria was one of Tia's favorite spots. She enjoyed the fresh air and scent of flowers when she came here to collect the spring drinking water required by her mistress.

"You said you brought word from my mother and father?" Tia's heart beat rapidly, and her body felt warm at speaking aloud about her parents.

"Yes," Malinche said as she settled into a comfortable position, smoothing her skirt beneath her legs. "They send their love and have a desire for you to know they are well. They miss you but are pleased to have a daughter serving in the house of the most powerful ruler of the nation. It is their source of pride."

Tia savored the words only a moment before speaking.

"But if they knew that Moctezuma is only powerful in his mind. In truth, he is fearful of losing this land to the Great White god," she said then slapped her hand against her mouth, appalled she'd spoken as boldly as Rebekha.

"Quetzalcoatl—the Great White God. I have heard of him," Malinche said, ignoring Tia's boldness.

When Tia saw no reproving look, she spoke again. "There is no such god. He is the imaginings of this weak and fearful ruler."

"You don't believe in him, then?" Malinche twisted a loose thread at the hem of her skirt as though she were distracted.

"My parents did not believe, so I do not believe. They are most wise in these matters." Her conviction did not waver in her voice.

Malinche smiled then said, "Your parents *do* believe."

She thought her heart had stopped completely. "My . . . they . . . *believe?*" She stared at the ground, fighting the thoughts and emotions that swirled around her mind. *How could they believe in this god?* All the gods she had seen worshiped in this great city believed in death and sacrifice. Her parents did not believe in the massacre of innocent souls at the whim of a god—any god. *And besides, there is no such thing as a white man.*

As though sensing her doubt, Malinche's gentle voice continued. "That is the message they sent with me. Your mother and father have listened to the words of a prophet and believe what he has said of the white god who will come. They want you to believe too."

31

A crazed thought wedged into Tia's head. *Have my parents become as disturbed as Moctezuma?* What did this news mean to her?

"They have asked that I share with you the message they have received," Malinche continued. "A great white god has once come upon this land, and Moctezuma or not, he will come again. They wish for you, their daughter, to seek and believe. And once you see the white god for yourself, either bring or send word to them. Can you do this?"

As though her head were no longer under her own control, Tia nodded, "Yes. Yes, I will wait and watch for the arrival of such a god, and once he has come, I will do all in my power to let my parents know." But, deep in her heart, she doubted she would ever have to carry through on her promise. A great white god indeed!

5

Three ships lined the dock, a flurry of men rushing about each of them, back and forth from the crates of supplies to the gangplank, loading supplies for the voyage. The screech of gulls and splash of water against the wooden bow seemed to add urgency to the shouts of the men. "Over here! Watch out below."

Felipe ducked as he walked around a dozen men hoisting barrels onto the deck of the largest ship in the harbor. His pace was bold as he scanned the area, seeking only one person among the active crowd—César. He must stop the marriage bands from going forth before César set sail. Not seeing him on the dock, Felipe started toward the boarding ramp where he recognized Miguel, his friend and ally in the youthful struggles against César.

Miguel stood beside a cask ready to be lifted by a rope pulley. Felipe watched his friend work and recognized why Cortés had chosen him. He was as strong as any man, and his patience was an added attribute. His youth gave him the energy to labor long hours, yet his temperament would keep him from refusing to follow orders.

"Miguel," Felipe called, stepping forward. Perhaps Miguel would know where to find César–and why the men were so furiously about their preparations when the launch was yet days away.

"My friend." Miguel opened his arms wide. "Who knows when we shall meet again?" They embraced as though this would be the last time they would ever see each other.

Offering a sharp smack of friendship against Miguel's back, Felipe pulled away. "Why are the men working on this day of hire? I thought there would be celebration."

"Haven't you heard?" Miguel asked, pulling a hank of rope from the ground and winding it around his forearm and shoulder. "Cortés has moved the launch to the morrow. He is already delayed a year due to a leg he broke when he fell." He lowered his voice and whispered as if he didn't want the other men working near him to hear. "Escaping from a clandestine visit from a lady's balcony, it is said." Miguel moved his eyebrows in a manner of conspiracy then continued, "And now there is a problem with Valesquez, the governor of Cuba. Cortés wishes to correct it immediately."

Felipe didn't care to hear more about the love affairs of Cortés, or his problems with the governor; he had a concern with his own. "Are all of the crew at the dock?"

"Yes." Miguel turned toward the ship and yelled at the man above, "All's secure." He stepped back, wrapping more rope onto his forearm as he watched the barrel begin to rise. Four men tugged against another length of rope attached to a block and tackle above the ship. Miguel steadied the barrel as it passed his head.

34

"Is César on a ship?" Felipe asked, indicating the entire fleet moored at the dock.

"He arrived moments ago and has gone on board." Miguel pointed to the ship where they stood. "I must go. There is much work to do." He stepped toward the next barrel, a nod of his head being his last farewell.

Felipe hesitated before approaching the ramp, his boldness of moments before suddenly vanished. He did not want confrontation with César but knew what he must do. Manuela's father had confirmed his fear. César had arranged for their marriage once this voyage was complete. The nuptial agreement was signed, the dowry payment made and already in the hands of César's dependant mother, a rare circumstance granted due to her needy situation. Unless Felipe could either get César to return the money, or he himself repaid the fund, her marriage to the hated César was assured.

"You will not marry Manuela," Felipe whispered, looking toward the ship where César would be. "I will stop you."

He pushed his way past the men who were still loading provisions, relieved no one tried to halt his search or question his presence. *If I look like I know where I am going, perhaps they will not notice me.* The ship was taller than the nearby Santo Domingo church, longer than the courtyard of the marketplace, and broader than the depth of the house where Felipe had grown up. If he hoped to find César quickly, he decided a systematic search of the ship would be best. Keeping to the edges, he walked the entire circumference of the upper deck.

Once he thought he saw César—the same sturdy build, powerful muscles in his upper arms, and shock of dark, unruly hair—but coming nearer, Felipe recognized Frederico Lopez. Frederico, only a few years older than he, had once lived nearby, but they had had little in common. He doubted the young man would remember him, but he didn't want to take a chance. Skirting around a mast to avoid any contact which might lead to his being recognized, Felipe did not speak to him, he did not dare. *If I am discovered, will I be escorted from the ship?*

Holding his face close against the neckline of his tunic, yet continuing to eye the faces of the laborers preparing the craft, he found that few of them seemed familiar—not a good thing for his continued anonymity. The search of the main deck proved fruitless, so he moved toward the narrow stairs which gave access to the lower levels. He prayed he would locate César before the ship sailed.

He heard César's voice before he saw him. "I am proud to be a member of your expedition, Señor Cortés."

Before reaching the stairs himself, Felipe spotted his adversary with the captain, coming up from below. Immediately, he stepped behind a stack of crates, not wanting a confrontation in front of Captain Cortés. From his hiding spot, Felipe could observe without César seeing him. Somehow he looked less formidable next to the Spaniard— César's stature more boyish, and his face pale compared to the dark beard which covered the face of the explorer.

"You will be an asset, I am certain," Hernán Cortés

said. His tone was curt, as if César were bothering him. "I must see that the food is being properly loaded into the hold. Stay here, boy, and help as these men need you."

Felipe took in the man's determined gaze, self-assurance evident beneath his heavy eyebrows; then he watched Cortés stride over the ramp to the dock below. He remembered the reason he stood on the ship's deck. César. He must talk with him, arrange the cancellation of the marriage bonds, and retrieve the dowry. If he were to marry Manuela, this last item was the most important of all.

Looking around, as though to observe the lowly men surrounding him, César took a seat on a nearby barrel.

Tired already? You've not even begun the work, Felipe thought. *Perhaps, a sign of laziness. That surprises me.* Taking advantage of his position and the idleness shown by the other lad, he moved behind the barrel César adopted as his resting place. No one seemed to care that both young men were not about the work that was happening around them, so Felipe closed his eyes, gathering his courage within him. With every tone of authority he could muster, he called, "César!"

César jumped from his seat, scanning the area to see who had addressed him. The men glanced but continued their work. Felipe stepped in front of César, anger evident through his rigid face and cold eyes. "Return the money to Manuela's father. She will not marry you. She will marry me."

Shaking his head, perhaps to clear his vision, as well as his emotion, César visibly relaxed. The line of worry left his brow and his shoulders relaxed. "Ha," he chuckled. "Why should I do that for you? For three years you have caused me shame. At last I may return the agony." He clenched his hands into fists, and leaned toward Felipe in the same gesture he had used so often as a boy hoping to garner authority over the others his age.

Felipe did not back down, squaring his shoulders. "What did I do to you?"

Again César moved closer, silently challenging him. "You brought me embarrassment by causing me to lose a race." He raised his fist then shook a pointed finger. "You are solely responsible for the laughter which has accompanied the memory."

"That was years ago, yet that is reason for you to take away the girl I have chosen to marry? I should be the one more offended." Felipe leaned toward to César's chest, returning the silent threat his proximity gave. "You bring *me* embarrassment by being one Cortés has chosen to go on this journey."

"I will make my country and my mother proud," César said. "I will make sweet Manuela learn to love me, erasing all my years of humiliation. Upon my return, I will marry her and remind you every day of the mistakes you made."

Felipe thought César had an odd way of trying to win her heart—one that would never succeed. Then realization washed over him. César was in love with Manuela. And she hated him. He spat at César's feet and stood tall. "You cannot make anyone love another. Manuela loves me. We will see who marries her."

Fire flashed in César's eyes, but Felipe continued. "Suddenly, I am glad it was you who was chosen to go. I will remain and earn enough money to buy out your dowry, marriage arrangement or not. Then Manuela will be my bride."

Felipe suddenly realized the other men had left the deck with their cargo, and the two of them were alone. He turned to leave also, but a sharp pain reached his thoughts before the sound of *crack* had settled into his ears. His vision narrowed. César stood above him, a wooden slat in his right hand. César dropped the board onto the barrel as Felipe crumpled to the deck.

"But you will not remain in Cuba," César said as he tugged Felipe toward the stairs and dragged him below. "Only as a worm within the lower decks of this ship, soon to be cast to sea like meat for the fish."

Felipe tried to struggle, to use his waning strength, then all went dark.

6

Manuela awoke early. The chirping tody outside her window insisted the day had begun. She rubbed her eyes and tried to locate the warbler in the dark. At last she saw the tiny bird, orange beak peeking through a woodpecker hole, red throat working to produce a song.

"You silly little thing," she said. "The sun is nothing more than a promise. It's not yet day." She kneeled at the window and tried to mimic the sound of the bird that was no larger than her thumb.

The tody continued its song until the sun began to rise. When the rays shone onto Manuela's face, warming the morning chill from her cheeks, she felt her stomach rumble.

"Time for me to leave you, Tody," she said, her chin resting on the window's ledge. The bright beams sparkled against the fine golden sand of the shore line not far beyond the garden. Manuela hesitated, drinking in the morning breeze as the sun rose higher. She could taste the saltiness of the humid air. The sweet smell of orchids tickled her nose.

When the light was no longer directly in her eyes, she stood, taking a final glance toward the horizon. A mast, full-sailed, moved across the blue sea. "Is a ship afloat so early from the harbor?" Then she noticed a second, and a third. She scanned north toward the docks. No other masts sliced the skyline.

"Cortés has sailed," she whispered. "The end of César." A smile played at the corner of her lips. "Felipe will repay the dowry. If he cannot, I will convince Papa that César's mother must return the payment. The engagement will be cancelled."

Manuela whistled a random tune as she changed into her day clothing of skirt and blouse, then moved into the common room where she gathered the morning meal. Placing slices of goat cheese and tortilla on crockery for both herself and her papa, she kept a smile upon her lips, knowing that all her plans could be accomplished, if only she had enough faith in Felipe. Or in herself.

A noise from the garden door signaled her papa's return. "Good morning," she greeted as he came in from the early feeding of the bulls. Already his brow was damp from his labor, and his shuffle said the day's heavy work had begun.

He nodded then sat to eat his meal. Her confidence waned at his silence. She wanted to talk about the dowry, but words would not come into her mind. She wanted to cry out, to tell her father she would not marry César, to scream at him that she hated César and loved Felipe, but nothing would be proper to say. Nothing that would not bring him

41

anger and hurt her cause. Bits and pieces of a one-sized conversation dashed through her mind. Several times she opened her mouth as though to speak, but no sound came forth. The only noise was the rhythmic pattern of his chewing. He was gone before Manuela could find the right words to speak.

By midmorning, Manuela finished her chores. She had thought Felipe would come early in the day to speak with her father. He had not, and she was disappointed. She sat near the window, making dainty stitches on a lace cloth she intended to use for her own home. Her stitches were not as steady as they had been yesterday, the day before the names were posted, the day before Papa had her betrothed to César, and the day before she worried if he would consider Felipe's attempt to change the bands that would lead her to an unwanted marriage.

The tody chattered again from outside. "Little bird," Manuela said. "How do you wait so for your mate to come home? Felipe is but delayed, and my heart is heavy with worry. I would not have the patience to sit upon my eggs as you will when the spring comes."

She placed aside her handwork, fearful the sewing she had done would need to be removed anyway, and stood at the front window, looking across the courtyard toward the docks. The masts she had seen this morning were no longer distant flecks against the blue. *Why hasn't Felipe come?* It was his absence that bothered her most, halting her concentration on the stitching, making her eyes drift toward the window and her mind wander to the ships that she had seen far from the harbor that morning.

"César will be gone many months. Felipe will have time to change Papa's mind. I must not worry that he comes so late," she said, trying to console herself. "I will be like the bird and wait most patiently."

But she was not patient as she paced the room, refusing to watch for Felipe. She picked up her lace but set it back down, still unable to concentrate. Her stitches had become crooked and uneven from worry. She reviewed the chores already completed, hoping something needed additional straightening or tending. She checked the pantry for a *bocadillo* roll, found one that wasn't stale, then adding *jamon* and cheese before nibbling at the bread.

When she could no longer stand the wait, she decided she would make her daily trip to the market. *Perhaps Felipe will be there. He might have found work. It will take no time for him to earn enough to repay the dowry.* She took a few coins from a jar in the pantry to cover any purchases she might wish to make then walked the short distance toward the city square.

On the way she passed a mule cart laden with intricately-crafted ceramic tiles bedded in lamb's wool to protect them. Manuela loved colorful tiles such as these that decorated the church where she and Papa celebrated mass. She stopped to run her finger against the raised texture. The inner circle was solid, and filigree patterns like waves and stars surrounded it for row after row, adding to the size of the artwork. *Much like my embroidery. Perhaps I can duplicate the pattern.*

"Can I interest you in making a purchase?" the elderly man who walked at the mule's lead asked as she passed.

"No, not today, Señor."

The smell of onions and sardines assailed her nose as she came upon the market. Manuela kept watch for Felipe while she looked over each trader's wares. She picked up a *naranja* and held it to her nose, drawing in a whiff of citrus through the deep orange peel. She placed it into her basket. She added lentils, red peppers, and *paella*. The rice would fill both their bellies and make her father sleepy for siesta. She gave coins to each merchant whose product she selected.

Manuela passed over the olives. Papa sometimes worked in the groves, and the December harvest had yielded enough of the green fruit to fill their larder. She would wait until she found Felipe before choosing either lamb or *chorizos* for dinner. She loved the little sausages served with a bowl of *gazpacho* and did not want them to spoil in the midday sun.

"Manuela!" She recognized Eduardo's voice. "Man-uel-a." His breath came in short spurts. He was running. He stopped in front of her and bent at his waist, hands on his knees as he gasped for air.

"Eduardo, why are you in such a hurry?" Manuela set her basket on the dirt beside her and held her hand toward the boy as if wanting to help him breathe.

"It's . . . Felipe," Eduardo said, continuing to pant.

She felt as if her heart dropped from its normal place into the pit of her stomach. "What is wrong? You must tell me." Her skin prickled, and her breath became ragged. She grabbed Eduardo's arm, hoping to hurry his answer.

He stood straight, pulling in two more deep breaths before he said, "No one has seen him since he went to look for César at the docks yesterday."

"Wha . . . surely someone has seen him." She felt cold pass through her where once had run warm blood.

"No one." Eduardo shook his head, took her hand then walked toward the seashore, away from the center of Santiago.

Manuela looked beyond him, beyond their path, toward the docks, allowing her suddenly tear-filled eyes to scan the ocean where she had last seen the masts. No masts were visible against the sky. They had been so far against the horizon this morning that she hadn't expected to see any, but she still was compelled to search for them.

Reaching the dock, the two of them stood in silence for a brief moment. At last, Eduardo spoke, his whispered message still cutting into her heart. "Manuela . . . he did not come home last night."

Her knees buckled beneath her, and her body slid toward the dock, the boards rough against her skin. She knew what Eduardo's next words would be. She would need strength. "Oh, Mary, full of grace, the Lord be with me."

Eduardo squatted beside her, his hand placed against her shoulder in a comforting gesture. "I've been to his house. His parents have not seen him since early yester-morn. A search has proved unfruitful. When I asked here at the docks, only one lad had seen him yesterday as he boarded Captain Córtes' ship. Felipe did not disembark before they set sail."

Tears poured from Manuela's eyes as the truth bore its way into her heart. "Bless me, dear mother." Was it possible? Had Felipe gone with Córtes after all? And what of César? Fear for Felipe's safety had never been greater than the immediate rush she felt at the thought perhaps César would do something to harm him.

"Let me help you home." Standing, Eduardo offered a hand, picking up her basket in the other. "I will do all in my power to find out where Felipe is. Do not worry."

She glanced toward Eduardo, unable to halt the tears. Her lips trembled, refusing to allow any words to form for several moments. How was she supposed to stop herself from worrying? Why hadn't Felipe come to tell her his plan? Why had she allowed him to leave her yesterday so abruptly?

"We will find him." Eduardo's soothing voice provided some comfort, and Manuela knew she could not simply remain at the docks, praying for Felipe's return. She placed her hand into the open one before her.

"I hope so," she whispered, at last coming to her feet to begin her journey. "I hope so."

7

The rhythmic swaying of the floorboards beneath him was too much for Felipe. Perhaps he would vomit if the rocking motion continued. He had to sit up, or the contents of his stomach might choke him, but his body would not respond. Fighting the bile rising in his throat, Felipe rolled onto his side to stop from swallowing the sour liquid if he lost the battle. A few deep breaths assuaged the churning.

Blinking his eyes did not hold them open. *I am so groggy.* Light trickled across his eyelids and warmed his cheeks. His eyes opened again and this time he was able to keep them that way for longer than a few seconds. Focused on the unfamiliar surroundings—huge crates, ropes coiled in bundles, bulging sacks—his mind worked to make sense. *Am I on a ship?* Felipe tried to see toward the dark edges. He was wedged between wooden crates near the back of the hold. *Jesu!*

"Why am I . . ." he said, then remembered his

conversation with César—"We will see . . ." Felipe touched a tender spot on the back of his head. *César could have thrown me overboard. And even though he hasn't, the crew may finish the job when they discover me.*

Felipe again tried to sit up, holding onto a crate for support. His entire body ached. *How long have I been unconscious?* The beam of light from the stairwell told him it was still day, but his stiff joints indicated he had lain in the same position for some time. *I must get off the ship.* As soon as Felipe thought it, he wondered, *or is this my chance to prove myself?*

Immediately, guilt swept through him. Manuela. He would marry her before César returned, despite the commitment her father had made in her behalf—*if* he were not too far from shore to swim to the mainland. *What if Cortés disposes of me as a stowaway?* If César didn't get to him first. *If . . .*

There were too many *ifs* in Felipe's mind.

He attempted to stand. The scene before him swam, his eyes blurry. His head throbbed, and his stomach churned. Seasickness or hunger? Every muscle in his body cried at the strain of movement. *How long have I been here?*

He noticed a crate of pineapples next to him, snatched one of the pieces of fruit and cracked it open, devouring the sweet yellow meat inside. The sticky juices ran down his hands and onto his arms, but he didn't care. The rumblings in his stomach subsided. He sat on a barrel marked *wheat,* until he felt control return to his legs. *Manuela . . .* What must she think with him suddenly gone? How long had it been? He had no way of knowing for sure.

Felipe stood at last by placing his hands against the wall. Working his way to the stairs, his sore muscles straining as he climbed one step at a time toward the light. The sudden brightness when he reached the upper deck nearly blinded him. He raised a hand to shield his eyes while he searched the horizon, hoping to see the shore, but finding no sign of land. He slumped against a mast, already defeated in his thoughts of returning home quickly to Manuela.

He had to rest for a moment. Finding César would come soon enough, perhaps before his body was recovered sufficiently to protect himself from his attacker. Members of the crew worked on the deck, tackling various tasks—pulling ropes, still moving crates and hauling sacks to the lower deck. The quick departure must have left the crew scrambling to get the supplies on board, leaving no time to finish their storage. Felipe moved away from the men, trying to keep his face hidden so no one would recognize him or sense that he didn't belong.

"Lend a hand here," one mate called, but Felipe pointed across the deck as if he had a job already awaiting him, then he ducked behind a mast. The sailor, his shoulders and head covered with a cloth that partially hid his face from the sun, made a grunt of displeasure and returned to his work.

None of the other men seemed to take notice as Felipe pulled an oblong piece of burlap cloth from the top of a stack of crates, and draped it across his head the same way the other man had done. Continuing to the back of the ship, Felipe looked hopefully into the wake that followed them. Ocean, ocean all around, all directions as far as his eye could see. The sky was clear blue, free of birds. Empty. No gulls flocked in search of tidbits left behind in the wake of the ship, a sure sign that they were a great distance from the shore.

He fought to hold back tears. His knees buckled. His emotions swirled from distress, to worry, to fear. Great beads of sweat burst across his forehead. What lay ahead? *Why did I ever want to come aboard this ship?* Would he ever return to Cuba, and Manuela? *If I had not come to find César . . .* Of course, his motivation was great. Finding César was the only way he could think of to remove Manuela from this unwanted promise of marriage and make her his own. And now César might take his life.

A burning rage grew within Felipe. He felt certain César had hoped him dead, not to return to Manuela. How many days before César would have thrown him into the ocean? Only the grace of God had prevented him from doing it before.

"César!" The booming shout snapped Felipe from his reverie.

"Yes, sir," he heard the all-too-familiar voice reply.

Felipe hid himself from view, crouching behind a barrel marked *gun powder.*

"Move this hemp below. It is in the way of the shipmen here on deck," a surly mate ordered.

César squatted to gather the ropes into his arms. The crewman backhanded his head, sending him sprawling.

"Let that be a lesson to you, lad, to anticipate the work that needs to be done." The man spat at César then stalked toward another group of sailors struggling with a crate.

Felipe had felt the power of the slap, but no pity—only dislike and distrust for César, who lay splayed across the pile, face down, legs tangled into the rope beneath him. The other men had moved away, leaving him alone with his enemy, still tangled in the rope. Overcoming his fear of similar abuse, Felipe strode to stand above César. *He thinks I'm a member of the crew.*

"Get up," Felipe commanded, enjoying the sudden position of power he held. If only he could maintain the upper hand.

César scrambled to regain his footing, his head bowed.

"How do I get passage back to Cuba?"

César jerked his head to look into Felipe's eyes. "You! I had hoped to toss your body overboard tonight. You have not stirred for almost two days."

Two days? No longer intimidated, Felipe's voice was stronger than his body felt. "You did not kill me, and I do not plan to kill you. But neither will I allow you to fulfill your dowry."

"You will not stop me," César said, sounding like he had in their village when he wanted the others to respect his power. He pulled his shoulders back and straightened his spine.

"Don't use that tone of voice with me again," Felipe said. "I am not afraid of you. You have met your match in the crewmen aboard this vessel." Standing his ground, his fists clenched, ready to respond, he allowed his eyes to look directly into those of his enemy.

"The men's power over me provides no safe haven for

you." César moved to strike, yet Felipe was too quick, and César's fist hit nothing but air.

"César!" The mate had returned.

Felipe lowered his hands and stepped out of the way. He covered a portion of his face with the cloth disguise.

César pointed toward him and yelled, "Stowaway!"

The sailor glanced but did not speak to Felipe, who stood tall to appear older. "Who cares?" He raised his hand to César's shoulder and gave him a shove. "Why is this rope still here? I told you to move it below."

"Yes, sir, but . . ." César struggled to keep his footing secure on the wet deck, his finger still pointing toward Felipe.

"There are no *buts* on this ship, lad," the mate said, his voice harsh. "You'll do as I say or you won't live to see the new continent." He slapped César hard, sending him reeling across the deck, fighting valiantly to maintain his balance. "Get it moved *now*." The man strode away.

César regained his footing before he picked up the rope. He paused directly in front of Felipe. A cold, hard look crossed his face. "I would watch my back if I were you," César said, his voice a growl. "I have made no foolish promises about sparing your life." He hoisted the rope to his shoulders and disappeared into the ship below.

A sigh coursed through Felipe's body as he stood alone at the rail, again watching the wake as the ship plowed through the water, away from land, away from Cuba, away from his beloved Manuela. *Oh, Manuela. How will I ever return?*

52

8

"She would never tell me I have done well. Queen Aramonia has forgotten all the manners she was taught as a child, the same ones she tried to teach me when she watched over me in my earliest years," Tia said as she and Malinche walked toward the *zócalo* square in the center of Tenochtitlan. Her eyebrows crinkled to match her frown and she remembered those days and wished their promise had come to a better end.

"You will be rewarded, for the service you give," Malinche said. "No master ever praises a slave, but your efforts will be remembered. Perhaps a gift of the freedom you so desire."

Tia considered Malinche's words, although she doubted their truthfulness. She had yet to observe anyone's effort being rewarded, especially not with freedom. The two girls continued walking, passing through the groups of slaves and traders who filled the streets, their carts jutting into the way, their voices loud. She followed this path many times on errands for Queen Aramonia. Today she had invited Malinche to come along and they were given permission.

"Don't you feel a warm glow within you when you have completed an especially difficult task?" Malinche stopped to consider a piece of fruit on a merchant's cart. "Banana. *Plátano dátil.*"

Tia tried the foreign words in her mind before answering Malinche's question. "I suppose so." She was startled and flinched away at the squawking of parrots clinging to a brace across the back of the next stall. Malinche giggled, and Tia joined in. "Parrot," she said the word as though it were foreign, then they both laughed again. "You know, Malinche, I often felt a warm glow when my mother gave me praise."

"That feeling is part of your reward."

Tia scrunched up her nose in distaste. "I can think of rewards I would rather have." They moved through the market again. Jewelry, pottery, and metalwork hung from carts in attractive displays.

"Name a reward," Malinche said. A slave bumped into her as the street narrowed, carts stationed on both sides.

Tia thought briefly. "Sleep."

Malinche laughed a full, rich sound. "In my study of the people of this land, I have learned a poem of their belief on this very subject. 'It is not true that we come on this earth to live. We come only to sleep, only to dream.'"

"Not in the palace of Moctezuma." Tia laughed at her own joke.

She stopped to purchase two *chicle*, popping one of the gummy wads into her mouth to chew. Malinche wandered on ahead. Until Malinche had arrived, Tia had not been happy, her tasks at the palace being more drudgery than interesting. No matter how hard the servants worked, the queen was rarely satisfied. She tried to please her mistress, but pleasing her could never be done. At least now she had a friend. She found relief by Malinche's very presence and hurried to catch up to her.

Malinche stood at the feather merchant's. "*Guacamayo.* Colorful." She held up a brightly colored flamingo plume against her charcoal hair. "Look, I'm the feathered serpent."

"Shhhh." Tia glanced around to see that no one had been close enough to hear her friend's words. "You will not want to mock the gods of Moctezuma where his priests might hear," she said, her warning voice hushed. "Moctezuma has great fear of the feathered serpent. He believes Quetzalcoatl will take away his power as ruler."

Malinche kept her voice low too. "What would he do if he heard me speak so?"

"Come," Tia said, as she walked. "You would be sacrificed to the gods. He believes the beating heart holds the most power. The priests strip the hearts from the honored victim at Moctezuma's command. They hold the heart above their heads, raising a chant as blood drips and runs down the temple steps."

Tia pointed toward the stone edifice, a pyramid which stood beyond the square. "The new temple of Huitzilopochtli. The Mejicas believe they were led to Tenochtitlan by Huitzilopochtli, the hummingbird god. He told them to search for a lake with a small island. When they saw an eagle eating a snake and perched on a cactus, they knew that is where they were to settle."

Malinche stared at the thousands of human skulls displayed on the *tzompantli* racks at the base of the temple. A gasp rose to her throat. She touched her hand against her breast. "Lake Texcoco fulfilled the prophesy?"

Tia nodded. "They believed, but the tribes already living there would not let them take the land, so the Mejicas created this city among the rocks and marshes. At first they traded with the others, but a desire for more land and riches caused them to overtake areas around them."

"This explains why they are constantly at war with the other settlements," Malinche said. Stepping away from the base of the pyramid, she lifted her face toward the sun, her eyes scanning the blood-marked stairs which led to the top of the sacred monument.

"Many more prophecies are yet to be fulfilled, just as there are more temples to other gods," Tia said. "According to another prophesy this year is designated for the return of Quetzalcoatl. Moctezuma makes sacrifices to please the god he fears will take over his lands."

"But doesn't Quetzalcoatl hate human sacrifice?" Malinche asked.

"To Moctezuma human sacrifice is the only action that will appease the gods—any god. He has executed generals, enslaved sons of lords, and called himself a god. Whether Quetzalcoatl accepts human sacrifice or not, Moctezuma cannot stop the pattern he wields as control over his people. No one is safe from his wrath. No one."

9

Every day Manuela went to the docks to watch the horizon. Other ships were moored in the slips, but the three ships of Cortés had sailed, and Felipe disappeared with them. A week had passed with no word. She had visited his home only to find that his mother grieved, but his father felt proud, believing his son must have joined the expedition after all.

In her heart, Manuela knew Felipe was on Cortés's ship. She could almost envision him standing on the deck of the now-gone main vessel once in the harbor, his hair blowing in the wind. The sounds of the crew of these new ships caused her to pause, checking faces with desire to see her love's among them. A flicker of white against the azure sky deep into the ocean gave her a moment's hope of a sail, but a gull wove through the clouds like a needle pulling thread through the pale fabric.

If he has sailed . . . she thought . . . *it was not his intent.* None of his belongings were gone from his room. He told no one he was leaving. *He would have come to me, unless he was dead.* No, she wouldn't think about that possibility. Her heart ached at his absence, even though a flame of hope remained that he would one day return. *Could César have anything to do with this?* Manuela refused to let her mind form any scene to answer the question.

She shielded her eyes against the sun. Stacks of lumber and ruined barrels lined the wooden dock. An abandoned anchor was skirted by odd ends of rope, and garbage skittered in the breeze along the gangway. The marine air was heavy, oppressing. Across the water, only the buoys sat low against the horizon. No mainsails dotted the seas.

Nothing.

"Manuela." It was Eduardo.

He had come up behind her but now stood at her side. A smattering of dirt streaked his cheeks amid the fuzz of his maturing beard. His eyes looked tired, as though he had not slept. *How faithful he has been to both Felipe and me.* She tried to smile, but her lips would not obey. She knew her eyes yielded the truth of sadness. She wrapped a tendril of hair around and around her forefinger. "No word?"

"We must believe he has somehow, for whatever reason, joined the expedition," Eduardo said. "Think how excited he must be to have this chance. It will be many months before you can expect him to return."

"Do you know how many? How long must I wait?" Manuela pulled the brightly-colored shawl around her shoulders as she sat upon a barrel on the dock. "I will remain faithful, no matter how long it takes." She shuffled her legs, settling in for the long wait and hoping to make her wooden seat as comfortable as possible.

Eduardo stepped toward her, tenderly touching her arm. "Manuela, be reasonable. Come to your home where you can be warm and safe."

"Is Felipe safe and warm?" She realized her tone was aloof, matching her spirit which had flown across the sea in search of her love, but she could not bring herself to listen to Eduardo's reason. The thought hurt too much, the loss of Felipe too recent. Workers passed between them, continuing to haul supplies toward boats moored at the docks.

"Felipe will take care of himself and no harm will come. I am jealous of what he will discover," Eduardo said. "Christopher Colón said the lands are the most beautiful that human eyes have ever seen, and the natives a gentle and trusting people."

"And his son, Diego Cólon, followed his father to ravage the treasures from the land. Is wealth a reason to perform ritual sacrifice, taking the lives of so many for the good of the king?" Her eyes scanned the water once again. A shake of her head confirmed she had seen nothing.

She jumped from her perch, walking toward the piazza in the city center, rebuilt after the great fire that had destroyed Santiago soon after its settlement. Eduardo followed her in silence. His countenance showed his confusion.

They passed noisy market stalls. Fruits and caged poultry were on display. Clothing and jewelry adorned the various carts. She stopped at one and held out a string of feathers. "These were taken back to Spain by the great explorer. For worthless trinkets, our Cuban motherland has lost hundreds of men."

"For more than trinkets, Manuela," Eduardo said, "for the exploration of new lands, finding new resources, and the thrill of discovery."

Manuela harrumphed, turned on her heel, and strode past the market, ignoring those who shoved other items—carved ships and bamboo, shell masks and vases—from the new lands into her path. Eduardo hurried to keep pace. At the steps of the church, she paused then asked, "Will you join me in prayer for the lost?"

"Felipe is not lost, Manuela." His voice was pleading as were his eyes. "Once the exploration is through he will return with Cortés. He will return to you."

"I want to believe that with all my soul," she said. "And that is why I pray every day for his safe return. Only through the grace of Mary will he be protected." She stepped into the cool recesses of the church, through the gold filigree which decorated the archway. Rows of benches led to the altar.

Eduardo hesitated before joining her.

She knelt, marble statues of Jesus and the Virgin a few feet from the altar. Candles flickered around the base of each figure. Manuela's head bowed, and she murmured a quiet prayer. Like the Madonna, she was a woman in her sorrow. Manuela felt a silent tear escape her eye and sketch a pattern on her cheek.

"Bring Felipe home safely," Eduardo whispered as a part of his own prayer. Hands extended, he mirrored the statue of the Virgin.

10

Felipe knew César would seek to do him harm. César never failed to fulfill a threat. This had been the case when they were children, and it would be no different when it came to Manuela and the marriage arrangement.

A half-dozen men were scattered across the deck. Two worked the ropes below the mast, another three were climbing the riggings, and one man was mopping the floor boards. No longer terrified of being discovered and tossed overboard by the crew as a stowaway, Felipe checked to see if Miguel was among them, but he was not. *I must find him. Perhaps he can help me return to Cuba.*

Hoping to keep the bright sun from scorching his skin, Felipe tightened the cloth headdress across his face once more. Another group of six men came onto the upper deck, tackling the remaining crates, ready to move them into the hold. Miguel was not among them either. Many sailors from the village had been listed with those Cortés chose for the journey, but Felipe did not recognize anyone.

"Give us a hand."

Felipe knew the order was directed toward him. Did he

dare join them, as if he belonged among the crew? When César had ratted on him, the shipmate had not reacted to his being a stowaway. Felipe wondered if those in charge would also ignore him if he joined in their work. The idea seemed better than trying to hide or avoid them until he could leave the ship, and if he didn't assist in the work, they might have even great cause to toss him overboard. Perhaps he would find Miguel more quickly by moving freely among the men.

He slipped into the group who were lifting a heavy crate marked *arma de fuego*. He strained to keep a grip on the rough surface. *Why do they need firearms?* And so many. He remembered seeing gun powder on the day the ships sailed. The danger he faced suddenly seemed more real.

"Above the shoulders, mates," a man called. He appeared to be in charge, perhaps a foreman. "One, two, three."

Felipe lost his footing as the box was heaved high then settled against the shoulders of the two lines of men. He regained his position but discovered the box did not touch his shoulder.

"Run along, lad," the foreman said a chuckle in his voice. "You'll be no use in carrying the load. Clear the way below for us."

Felipe scurried to the stairs, and yelled out the foreman's direct orders. "Clear the way below!" He hoped this order was loud enough to encourage anyone before him to move. He descended, and the men carrying the firearms followed.

He didn't know where the case was headed, so Felipe waited for the men to lead him through the storage areas. They worked their way deep into the underbelly of the vessel. He passed kegs of pineapples and recognized the hiding place César had used to hide him when he thought Felipe was dead. The darkness made it difficult for him to see. Once, tiny feet scurried across the top of his foot. Rats! The realization made him shudder, not from fear, but from the thought of sharing his sleep, and possibly his food, with the filthy animals.

At last they reached their destination, and Felipe stepped forward to help balance the load as it was lowered onto the floorboards. The men stood rubbing their arms and shoulders, trying to work out cramps from the weight.

"Only four more to go, men," the foreman said.

The men moaned as they lumbered toward the stairs again. He joined their progress and made sure the passageway was clear each time. Other men, involved in their own ship assignments, respected his orders and hurried from the stairwell as the loads passed through.

When the job was done, the men Felipe had been helping scattered, and he headed topside himself. He'd still not found Miguel, and his hope was wearing thin. The sun poured into his eyes, so Felipe held his hand above his eyes, shading them enough that he could see as he turned in a circle to check once more for Miguel.

At his final turn, the foreman, his hands resting on his hips, stood before Felipe. "What's your name, son?"

Felipe had thought he was alone. His heart raced, not only from the work he had been doing, but also out of fear.

"I know you are not the boy *César.* Are you Miguel?"

This might be a way to escape penalty for being aboard ship without cause, but he didn't want to get Miguel into trouble, either. *What will this man do to me if I'm not Miguel?* "I . . . no, I am not Mig—Miguel," he said, stammering. *Why did I think he wouldn't notice?* Felipe thought he might vomit, his head felt light while his worst fears came rushing back, exploding within him.

The man waited.

"My name is . . ." Felipe felt beads of sweat along the edge of his scalp. He had no other choice but to tell him. "My name is Felipe Marco."

The foreman smiled broadly. "Well, Felipe Marco, I don't know how you came aboard this vessel, but welcome."

Welcome? Relief washed over him, the worry suddenly calmed. "We can use another hand, and a lad as slight as you won't eat much. Besides, we already lost one man who fell from the sails and found his bed in the sea."

Oh, my Lord . . . Felipe's worry rushed back upon him, but the foreman continued.

"Join the others on the lower deck for a meal then find me on top, and I'll give you more work to do." He gave Felipe a solid pat on the back before walking away.

"Gracias." Pushing the idea of falling overboard from his mind, he regained calm as his heart rate returned to normal. He almost couldn't believe that this man, too, had released him without any repercussions. Felipe hurried in the direction the other crew members had gone, taking the stairs two at a time to the level below.

The area was broad and open, except for the occasional pole which supported the weight of the upper decks. Long, rough-hewn planks served as tables for the nearly two hundred men seated along each side. A sea of men. *I'll never find Miguel*, he thought.

Platters of food circulated among the tables as he scanned the faces for yet another time this day, hoping to see one he knew. The torches cast dim light within the room. The opened hatches provided more, but the ruddy skin and dirty faces of the men hid much of their unique features. At last, his hunger overtook him, and he rushed to a seat, grabbing a chunk of meat as the plate passed by. He shoved the piece into his mouth and chewed. *Heaven.* A lone banana was on the table, and he picked it up as well. The peel fell away and the sweet fruit was devoured. His stomach only roared for more. Felipe used the ladle to fill his plate with stew, reached in front of a crewman to tear a wad of hard-crusted bread from the long loaf on a platter, and accepted a pint of *guaro*—the sweet flavor like sugar on his tongue—from a man who passed the *jarro* among the seated crew.

When at last his plate was empty and his hunger sated, Felipe looked again at each man who sat around him. He recognized Herberto Guzman's father and thought he saw Carlos Limian, a young man from near the olive groves above Santiago. None of the others seemed familiar. To his relief, César was not among them, but he wished Miguel had been.

He patted his full stomach, pleased by the resounding

belch that came from deep within. Never had a meal tasted so good. Not even a meal set by Manuela—excellent cook that she was—had ever delivered food that tasted as good as this one did at this moment, although he did love the chorizos sausages she served with a bowl of gazpacho.

Manuela was . . . Manuela was . . . across the sea. Home in Santiago. The place where he should be. A realization struck Felipe. This was not the way his life was meant to be. This ship, these men, this journey was not what he wanted. Why had he ever sought adventure and to leave Santiago? What he wanted was to be with Manuela, to be her husband, to wake up every day and look upon her face. Now his greatest fear was that he would never leave this ship and make passage home. *I'll never see my sweet Manuela again.* No matter what, this could not be.

11

Before they left the market, Malinche exchanged a few cocoa for a gold arm band designed with two finely turned cords, bound together, twisted to link into one. "In memory of our friendship," she said as she handed the trinket to Tia.

"Gold cannot replace your presence," Tia said.

"You have taught me much about the value of friendship. I will miss you," Malinche said.

"And you have taught me about service, language, and the great white god of culture and learning. You've shared stories from my parents who told you of his ancient visit to our ancestors. Perhaps someday I will again see my parents—and perhaps I too will believe."

"I hope you continue to read and study. Listen to the words of the merchants in the square, and the languages will come easily. The histories teach much about your ruler and his mistaken beliefs. It is appropriate that he lives in Tenochtitlan, the city where men become gods." Malinche's familiar chuckle followed her words. "He has many gods to worship."

"Moctezuma fears the power of the gods, so he worships them all," Tia said. "The temples he has built in Tenochtitlan are proof of that. How will I know which beliefs are right?"

Malinche patted her hand. "As you learn, the truth will come into your heart."

She wished she knew more about the prophecies, but their conversation did not deeply explore any of them. Malinche told her first about the three-headed star streaking across the sky like a set of *quauhololli*, each weapon's head attached to a single club. Then she reminded Tia that last year the earth had shaken in an omen of Quetzalcóatl's coming, loosening stones from the temple of Xiuhtecuhtli, crushing a child in their wake.

"Merchants were thrown to the street. Even the temple walls in Malinalco moved enough to crack in several places," Malinche said. "And now, it is the promised year for his return—CeAcatl, the Year of the Single Reed."

"But the prophesies *are* being fulfilled," Tia insisted. "The thousand stones rained from the sky on generals and troops in the battlefield."

"Warnings have come before with the seasons of the calendar," Malinche said. "Remember the tales of childhood, and the story of the forty nights an unknown light burned on the horizon? The light came back a second time, but no harm came from it. One day the complete prophesy may indeed come true." Malinche lowered her voice, as if she were spilling a great secret. "But perhaps not this time. Watch, listen, learn."

Tia vowed she would follow Malinche's advice. She would learn the histories, language, and beliefs of these people, then listen to her heart and know the truth.

The rain this morning seemed no more gentle than the rain of a thousand stones the soldiers had felt. She would live through this, too. Tia replayed the conversation she had had with Malinche in her mind as she watched the raindrops which had started before dawn. It was summer, the season for showers that often lasted throughout the daylight. Soon the god Tlaloc would cause floods to wash across the lands, destroying crops, displacing homes, drowning unwary people.

The god of rain demands the sacrifice of too many, she thought. But which of the gods did not? She stood from her sleeping mat, and padded toward the window. Already the air seemed thick and oppressive. Six days without sun. Six days since Malinche had said she would be traveling again with the trader, Iccauhtli. Six days her heart had been heavy because her friend was leaving. After today she might never see Malinche again.

She rolled her mat, dressed, and walked down the hallway toward her mistress's rooms. No candle burned at Aramonia's bedside. The woman must have been soothed by the rhythm of the storm, sleeping later than she might on another day.

Slipping back into the halls, Tia moved toward the servant's kitchen. A bustle of activity engulfed her the moment she passed through the door.

AMalinche and Iccauhtli depart today," Jeroni said as she reached for Tia's arm, pulling her toward the pot boiling over the open flames of the cooking pit. "Stir this bowl of corn-meal."

Tia took the ladle and began the task. The thick batter would have a sweet flavor; the aroma was of chili peppers. Jeroni kneaded dough, forming it into round balls the size of a kukui nut then pressing it against her palm to flatten. Rebekha stood at the table, chopping avocado, tomatoes and squash to add to the tlaxcalli wrap Jeroni was making.

Spooning the atolli into a bowl, Tia added pieces of lime to the mixture, something her mother had taught her to add zest to the dish. "Will Malinche eat with us before her journey begins?" Tia knew her voice was pleading. This last time she would ever saw her friend.

"Am I not here?"

A quick turn and she saw Malinche, her cotton blouse and skirt the same ones she had worn the day of her arrival. She took the bowl from Tia and sprinkled grains of maize onto the gruel. Rebekha set a clay griddle stacked with tlaxcalli in the center of the table. Jeroni added a bowl of black beans, and Tia brought the atolli.

The room became quieter than she ever remembered for a meal before, as though each of the women had gone mute. She knew the reason because it was also her own. This was the last meal with Malinche, a woman they had all grown to love. No one wanted to miss anything she might say.

They ate in silence for some time. When at last Malinche finished her food, she turned to Jeroni. "I will miss the meals you have prepared while I have been here. Nowhere have I tasted fruit more sweet, grains more rich, or meat more fresh."

The cook, pleased with the compliment, nodded. Rebekha stood to remove the plates from the table.

"Sit for a moment," Malinche said, reaching out to touch the girl's arm. Rebekha did as she was asked, and Malinche cleared her throat before continuing. "Once I heard a wise man say: 'Does man possess any truth? If not, our song is no longer true.'"

The young woman looked at each of the others seated around her, stopping her gaze on Tia.

Truth. Indeed, that is what I am seeking, Tia thought.

Malinche began again, reciting a poem Tia had heard somewhere before. "One day we must go, one night we will descend into the region of mystery. In peace and pleasure let us spend our lives; come, let us enjoy ourselves. Would that we lived forever; would that one were not to die!"

"'Would that we lived forever,'" Rebekha said.

"Forever," Tia added. "Would that we were all together forever as well." She stood and stepped toward Malinche, who pulled her into an embrace, not unlike the one her mother had given when she left home for Moctezuma's palace.

Then Malinche was gone.

71

12

Manuela listened to the afternoon shower beating against the ceramic tiles within the garden. She knew that the rain would soon stop; it always did in the early summer. In weeks hence, the storms might continue on, drenching Santiago and battering the ships in the harbor. But for now, the morning rains only freshened the air and watered the crops.

Each day, her life droned on steadily like the beating droplets. She rose early to prepare a meal for Papa before he went to tend bulls or to work in the fields. She finished whatever household chores that must be done, then prepared a mid-day meal for both of them to eat before her papa went to his afternoons with the sheep. That was usually when Manuela went to the docks to question the workers and gaze toward the horizon where she hoped Cortés and his ships would return. Today she'd wait for the rain shower to stop, but the delay was almost more than she could bear.

Eduardo wouldn't be at the docks during the storm, so there was no purpose in going yet. Instead of watching the tide and praying for the miracle of a ship's mast upon the horizon, Manuela wanted to discuss her plan with Eduardo. Her father had delivered a dowry to César, which he'd then given his widowed mother. If she hoped to cancel the promise, Manuela had to repay the amount to her father. She no longer wanted to wait for Felipe to take care of her. Her freedom was her responsibility. She was certain when the money was returned the marriage bands would not be sealed, and Papa would be made t listen to reason.

In those first days after the ships sailed, Manuela had tried to convince her father that she could not marry César.

"The arrangements are made, the dowry payment accepted," Papa had said. "There will be no change."

"But, Papa," Manuela had said. "I do not love César— "She had stopped at the flash of anger in her papa's eyes.

"It is a better match." He left the room, the conversation over.

His clipped words had cut her heart like the sharp leaves of the sugar cane against her tender skin. She knew there was nothing more that she could say. Instead, she continued to pray Felipe would return safely. *Felipe, I still wait for you, as I promised.* Perhaps her thoughts would carry across the distance between them. No such prayers of safety were offered for César.

In all the weeks which passed, she had not failed to make a daily trek to the docks. She asked everyone time and again if they remembered anything from that last day, the day Felipe disappeared.

"Did you see Felipe Marco on the day the ships sailed?"

The answer was always the same.

No one had seen him since he had been in the courtyard. None remembered anything significant. One had seen him walking toward the docks; another thought he had gone toward the ruins from the great fire. Nothing had been proven, despite her efforts to do so.

And time continued to pass.

Today was her birthday, but Manuela felt no desire to celebrate. In all of Santiago de Cuba, no one was more concerned than she—not even Felipe's parents. Certain now their son had joined Cortés, pride filled both their hearts, and they were content to wait until he returned.

"Felipe is a good boy," his mother had told her. "He would not leave except to join Cortés. I pray he will return when the explorer does."

Manuela prayed Felipe's mother was right.

Most of the other girls of sixteen were preparing for marriage, and Manuela was tired of waiting. She tried to ignore the signs around her that time was slipping away. Instead of the eggs the mother bird had once sat upon, tiny chicks now opened their mouths, seeking food. The olive harvest had passed, and her papa had more time to dedicate to calving. The sweet-smelling jasmine blooms opened, their fragrance permeating her bedroom. They reminded her of the time Felipe didn't recognize the blooms as anything more than weeds, chopping them off before they had time to open. A bittersweet smile crossed her lips.

If only her mother were alive, Manuela might have been able to choose a husband. But her papa believed in the traditions of their ancestors, the early conquistadors and colonists from Spain. Arranged marriages were sacred and an honorable trust, but to her love was more important. She would *not* marry César!

She had spent the previous night thinking about the things she would need to set up a home for herself—and Felipe. She wanted to be prepared to marry him the moment the ships returned. And now, she had plans of her own. Manuela intended to save enough to satisfy the debt to her father. Few women in Cuba ever earned wages on their own, living instead on the kindness of their husbands, or the pity of neighbors. She could not beg in the streets, bringing dishonor to her papa. Only dark-skinned slaves edged the markets, offering themselves in exchange for coin. *I could never do that!* The shame would be too great to again face Felipe, no matter the reason behind her actions.

The idea had been born that, rather than staying each afternoon at the docks searching the horizon, she might better use her days engaged in work which would bring money. Needlework was her mother's legacy. Manuela remembered the hot afternoons spent at her side, dutifully practicing the tiny, regular stitches.

"You have learned well," her mother had told her. "Your needlework is beautiful, among the best I have seen. Queens would be honored to wear a piece you have embroidered."

They were among the last words to Manuela from her mother before the sickness took her. The words were as treasured as the memories. "Perhaps there are no queens in Cuba, but surely the women at the marketplace would be willing to pay something for my work," Manuela said, convincing herself she must try.

Now if she could persuade Eduardo to help her. He could sell her wares at the market. It was common for boys to approach women in the marketplace, offering bargains unavailable in the merchant stalls. She would pay Eduardo a portion of the price, hoping he would negotiate a fair sum for her effort.

One coin at a time, she thought. *Every one I save brings me that much closer to my freedom.*

If only the rains would stop . . .

13

Felipe lost count how many days the fleet had been at sea. Time passed in a routine. Awake at dawn, eating gruel and dried fruit to begin the day, meals for mid-day and evening, working steady throughout his shift—he was assigned to scrub the decks—and falling in a death-like sleep at the end of each day. He was glad he'd been ordered work on the upper level where he could enjoy the sunshine and warm breezes across the tropics. The ship's maintenance work continued days after day, and only after the evening meal was he free to search the ship for Miguel.

Time passed with no sign of him, and Felipe continued to avoid César. It was not hard to recognize him in the midst of the other men. His stocky build kept him assigned to the crews responsible for hauling and lifting, and his strength was well-tested, although he was not quite as tall as the others. Felipe's chores on deck did not often place them on the same path. If only he could locate Miguel. There were over two hundred men on this ship, and Felipe had looked carefully at every one, it seemed, with no luck.

Until now.

The line for the mid-day meal was slower than usual, an argument happening between two crew members over a plate of biscuits. The previous shift of men remained seated, apparently curious about the outcome of the situation, as the new group—the one Felipe had joined—waited for the line to again move forward and the seats to open for them. The extra time, and the presence of additional crewmen all in one place, allowed him to peruse the weather-worn, tired faces at a more leisurely pace than usual. At last a foreman stepped between the two men who were arguing, cuffing one in the ear and sending the other sprawling across the floor, and the line began to move.

Felipe took advantage of the scuffle, drawing an extra portion of beef from the cook, taking a seat as the previous occupant vacated one, the entertainment over. As he ate, he kept his eye upon the remaining men passing through the meal line, spotting Miguel as the final man was served. He jumped from his spot on the bench, rushing across the room, calling, "Miguel!"

Miguel turned to face him. "Felipe?" His voice carried his wonder as to how and why Felipe was on the ship.

"I thought I would never find you," Felipe said as he caught up to where Miguel stood at the end of the line. He clung to him in embrace, as if Miguel were a rope tossed to a drowning sailor. After a second, he stepped back, looking into the face of his friend.

"How did you . . . Where have you . . ." Miguel didn't finish his questions, confusion evident in the furrow of his brow. "Last I saw, you were at the dock searching for César."

They moved forward, allowing Miguel to get his food then Felipe guided him to the long table where his own plate remained. "Let's sit where you can eat. I will tell you everything. I am so glad to have found you and that my life has been spared."

Miguel's interest was shown in the way his eyes opened wide and his mouth formed an O. "Tell me." He tore a chunk from his bread, placed it in his mouth, and began to chew.

"On the day Cortes posted the announcement seeking men to join this expedition, like everyone else, I added my name to the list," Felipe began. Miguel listened intently to the recounting of events that had led Felipe to the ship, and how he awoke in the hold. He told of his quest to locate Miguel without crossing César's path again.

"It is a wonder you are here, and a miracle that César did not dispose of you," Miguel said. "Now that the head mate knows you are among us, surely César will not be able to harm you."

Felipe took another bite of his own food before speaking. "But safety does not take me back to Manuela."

"Not yet, my amigo, but the journey from Cuba is done. Our time at sea is nearly-over."

Felipe's face showed his surprise, his eyebrows forming two questioning arcs above his wide eyes.

"The signs are there," Miguel said. "I spotted a bird on the horizon yesterday when I was aloft in the crow's nest. I didn't tell anyone because I wanted to be sure. Tomorrow—tomorrow we complete the first leg of our journey."

"And soon I will go home to Manuela," Felipe said, a sigh of contentment following his words. The last sign of worry passed as his heart swelled with the spirit of adventure. His love for Manuela was true, and he would return to her, but he had time to complete this adventure. César was on the ship and could not take her away any longer. Manuela had surely guessed what had happened to him and knew he would return. This would be his way to his prove worth to her father. Felipe would take Manuela as his bride and offer her riches far and above what César was paid as the dowry.

She would become *his* queen. He prayed that Cortés would conduct his exploration quickly so they could once again be in the ships, headed toward home.

But Cortés did not see his exploration that way.

Over the next few months, Cortés made several stops in his course, taking a crew aboard a sloop and leaving the massive ships—with Felipe aboard one of them—far from shore, and even farther away from his Manuela.

The constant delays were nearly more than Felipe could stand to bear, yet he had no other choice. Cortés was in charge of this expedition, not Felipe, and there were no ships to take him back to the homeland of Cuba without Cortés.

Days slipped into weeks, and the dangers they faced increased, but still he kept the faith that he would one day return home and marry Manuela.

14

Kneeling at the water's edge, Tia dipped the garment then gently wrung the fabric before setting it onto the pile of cleaned clothing. *Perhaps I could buy my freedom,* she thought, picking up the next item. But she knew the impossibility. Slaves had nothing of value with which to barter, and she could not risk stealing the cocoa beans used in exchange for goods. She feared the punishments Queen Aramonia might inflict—would she dare going so far as a beating of her personal slave?—if each bean were not accounted for from the market. She twisted the material in frustration.

Her desire to leave the palace had grown deeper as she investigated the teachings of the Feathered Serpent— Quetzalcoatl, the god of peace, so unlike the supreme ruler of this land, Moctezuma. *Moctezuma—He who frowns like a lord, pierces the sky with an arrow.* His name grew more meaningful as he offered sacrifice from the top of the temple, hoping the slaughter would prevent his overthrow. Would he now look within the palace for martyrs? Her heart twinged with fear. If the queen thought she was hiding the cocoa, would she send her to Moctezuma as a sacrifice?

Perhaps the gods were not pleased by his using conquests as a sacrifice. Surely Quetzalcoatl was not as fearsome as this ruler. Although Tia believed the history of the god, she doubted prophesy that he would return this year. The Year of the Single Reed was indeed upon the land. It had come every fifty-two years of the Xiuhpohualli without the white god returning. Over three generations, people had looked for him, but in the end, nothing. After all, prophesies could be interpreted as the priests so desired.

Gathering the washing, she started toward the courtyard. As she passed the bench where she had first spoken with Malinche, she worked her mouth in silence and practiced the foreign words she had learned from the cultured slave. *Banana. Mango.* She avoided the other women who carried out their own work, drawing water from the well or hurrying back from the river with arms loaded with clothing as she was.

"Tia, you must come," Rebekha called as she passed. The young girl's arms were empty, and her voice had the hush of an important secret. "Our guards report mountains that move on the sea."

"Another sign of Quetzalcoatl?" Tia chuckled at what she felt was her own joke. She had started paying closer attention to the stories told by Jeroni, the cook, about the last Year of the Single Reed, tales learned from Jeroni's grandmother. One had included a mountain that moved.

Rebekha stopped at the threshold. "Not a sign. Quetzalcoatl himself. A messenger has brought paintings of a strange man with white skin and dark hair upon his face."

82

"There is no such person," Tia said.

"You know the omens," Rebekha said. "Today prophesy is fulfilled."

Tia did indeed know the omens and the interpretation Moctezuma's advisers had given. Eight omens had appeared to the people of Tenochtitlan, each foretelling the coming of the white god.

Nearly the entire year after Tia had come to live at the palace, a great column of fire burned over the city. The bright streak of flame with a forked tongue had speared the night sky, only to be overcome each morning by the sun. She remembered how frightened she had been—how scared everyone had been—the first few times. What did the forked tongue mean? And, because the sun was the source of all life, what would happen if it failed to rise one morning? As the days passed with the fire growing no closer, her heart settled and the fear wore away. One night, the flame was gone.

A few months later, the first temple of Huitzilopochtli burned down mysteriously. Had there been lightning, as hit the temple of Xiuhtecuhtli, Moctezuma might not have feared this omen, but the night sky had been clear.

Then the fire was back. This time it came during the day, in three parts, streaming through the sky. Its brilliance diminished even the rays of the sun.

"The gods would destroy my city!@ Moctezuma had cried.

She feared Moctezuma would do a faster job on his own.

But the gods were not done yet. Last year Lake Texcoco

had boiled and flooded, destroying homes and burying people. A weeping woman was heard during the night, crying for the Mejicas to flee the city. A strange ashen crane appeared. Tia had heard the rumors that through a mirror in the crane's head Moctezuma saw the stars, and when he looked again, he saw a land where men rode on the backs of animals and fought against each other. Large, deformed men with two heads ran through the streets but disappeared when they were brought to Moctezuma. He decided surely these omens pointed the same direction—toward the white god.

"Quetzalcoatl has arrived," Rebekha said, interrupting Tia's memories. "There is a painting. Come see for yourself."

"Who are these men?" Tia asked, not believing her friend's interpretation.

Until she could see it with her own eyes, she would not trust that a man's skin could be white instead of copper like her own. Her entire life had been spent denying the possibility that a white god had not only come, but would someday return. Now Rebekha had invited her to see for herself. Did she dare? Would she see a white man, even if she believed such a person did not exist? The possibility shook the core of her belief.

15

"Land! Land!" called Miguel who was aloft, keeping watch. The shoreline, a white sandy beach brilliant against aqua waters, formed a thin bridge across the horizon. The land this time not only looked different, but Cortés seemed to be approaching a landing, not like his forays onto land before. They had left Port Santiago de Cuba in November. It was now July. Seven long months it had taken to again land. Some of the crew had become disgruntled over the time that had passed, and Felipe was tired of what he viewed as too great a delay.

Yet, despite his unhappiness at being away from his sweet Manuela, he still found himself excited to be a part of the adventure. The sea air was warm as the three main ships neared the shore. Eight brigantines, used throughout the journey to carry supplies, followed behind. Cortés said he hoped to use them to bring riches back to Isabella, his queen. The leader stood at the helm, holding his standard of black velvet, declaring his confidence that this new land would soon belong to his homeland, with he himself as the conqueror. The words embroidered in gold above a scarlet cross on the banner read: *Friends, let us follow the cross, and under this sign, if we have faith, we will conquer!*

The crew paused to gaze at the expanse before them. Felipe joined them at the ship's railing. He scanned the line to make sure César was not among those close to him. How he had avoided an encounter all these months had been a gift from god, Felipe thought.

As the ships neared the coast, several canoes came toward their fleet from the shoreline. Darkened skin and unusual dress—loin cloths and feathered headdresses—told him the men aboard were natives.

"Drop the anchors," Cortés ordered the foreman.

"Drop anchor," the sailor called, and the message was repeated from the other ships that were part of their company.

Felipe gave a hand to the nearest crew member, the two of them pulling the rope from its mooring and letting the twine ease between each of their fists. A splash, and the iron was overboard. The ship stopped its forward movement. As the other vessels dropped anchor, it caused a gentle rocking of the ship from the waves.

"Lower the ladder," Cortés ordered as the canoes drew near.

With them was a young woman who appeared to be not much older than Felipe. She spoke to Cortés, and he motioned for both she and the men she was with to board the boat. Felipe was surprised to see César step up to guide the party toward Cortés. The woman stayed near the leader of the natives. The visitors dropped to the deck, kneeling at the conquistador's feet.

One man spoke as he rose and offered a serpent mask to Cortés. The woman gestured and spoke, using a few words near enough to his own, with hand motions that Felipe was able to understand. "Gifts . . . servant . . . Moctezuma . . . guards kingdom . . . safe for your return." She stepped away from the native leader.

The conquistador seemed unsure what to do as he stood holding the turquoise-covered piece, while the man draped gold and jade bands around Cortés's neck. Another native placed a headdress of blue-green feathers on the Spaniard's head, an ocelot skin cape around his shoulders, and glistening black obsidian sandals on his feet. He was adorned with bands on his wrists and ankles. So much was going on around him that it was hard for Felipe to take everything in.

Additional natives from the canoe handed a steady stream of gifts to crew members standing near Cortés. Serpent-head spears and staffs inlaid with green jade, shields, fans heavy with gold and turquoise, and more masks were distributed, passed to the crew members of Cortés's ship. One of the fans was handed to Felipe who slipped it into his tunic, surprised, yet pleased, to be included in the receiving of gifts. *Something to take home to Manuela.*

When all of the items from the canoes had been given, Cortés looked at the man who had first spoken and asked, "Is this all you have brought?"

Again the young woman translated the man's reply. "Yes, lord. This is everything."

"Place manacles around their ankles," Cortés ordered.

A dozen men jumped to follow his command as the natives' faces showed confusion. Felipe fought to sort out what was happening. Why would Cortés accept these gifts then order the givers to be manacled? Had the man gone mad? Cortés gazed toward the shore where additional warriors waited for the return of their canoes. He certainly didn't seem to have his wits about him as he sent the next order.

"Fire the cannon."

The blast was shocking even to those who had heard the sound before. To the natives, it was devastating. They fainted.

16

Tia continued her work in Aramonia's quarters while listening to the conversation the queen was having with her husband.

"We still do not know if the visitors are divine or mortal," Moctezuma said, his concern evident in his voice. "They sit upon huge deer which carry them wherever they want to go." He paced the room, massaging his hands into his cheeks, fingers kneading his forehead.

Queen Aramonia stepped toward him, taking his hands into her own. "Do you think he will accept the gifts?"

"Who would not accept gold and silver? But will gifts delay these men or prevent them from overtaking our city?"

Fascinated, Tia hoped Moctezuma would not send her from the room. He would do anything, even appear to bow down to the great white god, if he thought doing so would protect his position as supreme leader.

"The gods will uphold your leadership, my husband,"

the queen said as she nuzzled against his chest, her right arm wrapped around his waist. Moctezuma lowered his face toward that of his queen, rubbing his lips against her cheek. The conversation seemed to be over, so Tia slipped from the room.

She doubted a true god would believe the ruler's insincere compliance, instead seeing the inner workings of this man who sacrificed others by the thousands for his own purposes. Word had already come from Moctezuma. The palace must be readied. She had received specific instructions from Queen Aramonia regarding clothing to be prepared, sleeping rooms to be arranged, and expensive foods to be purchased. It seemed everyone had more than enough to do before the strange, bearded man and his armies entered Tenochtitlan.

Tia traveled familiar streets, crossing the single canal on her way toward the market square, a memorized list of purchases to make and more cocoa beans in her money purse than the queen had ever entrusted her with before. *Perhaps I can practice the language I learned from Malinche,* she thought. For a moment, the memory of the beautiful slave girl saddened her heart. She missed her friend, the times they had laughed together, the secrets they had shared. No matter that Malinche had been at the palace only a short time; Tia felt an instant connection with the girl. She trusted her, even the message she had brought regarding her own parents believing in the great white god. She couldn't stop herself from wondering yet again, if her parents believed, then perhaps the message is true.

90

Many people gathered near the temple where she and Malinche had discussed human sacrifices and religion. The cultured slave had shared precious details about the white god who had visited the lands many years ago, bringing a message of peace. He had warned them to beware of false prophets.

"I know of no false prophet so grand as Moctezuma," Tia had said.

"And perhaps those who guide him," Malinche added. "To have many false prophets means there must be one who will be true, doesn't it?"

Tia had been forced to agree, and she was certain Malinche also believed in the white god and his teachings. There was no good without bad, no right without wrong. Opposition was necessary in all things. Did this mean if some skin was dark, there could also be skin that was light? Possibilities swarmed in her mind as she entered the marketplace. She had never seen it so crowded. The usual vendors lined narrow alleys into the open square. More dotted the plaza. Slaves like herself bartered for trade, arm baskets filled with goods. But today, priests, warriors, and even leaders from Moctezuma's royal courts mingled among those gathered to do their daily business.

The painting, she thought. *These people must have come to view the portrait of the bearded man. The white man.*

Tia worked her way toward the linen merchant. Queen Aramonia desired a new garment for the white god's arrival at Moctezuma's door. She selected fabric like the queen demanded. "Softer than the fur of a kitten. Smoother than the cheek of a babe."

"Moctezuma has sent a brigade to the far water." The woman standing in front of Tia spoke to the merchant as their currency exchanged hands.

"So I have heard," the merchant said. "The Totonacs have already met with the white god and joined forced with him. Moctezuma fears they will turn the heart of the god against our people."

"Moctezuma has turned the heart of all the gods against his own people," the woman said, a bitter laugh in her voice.

If only this were a situation to laugh about. Tia agreed with the woman; the gods were not favorable toward the Mejicas. When the woman finished her purchase, Tia moved forward to pay for Queen Aramonia's fabric.

"Have you seen the painting?" the cloth merchant asked Tia as he wrapped her package and handed it to her. She shook her head. "Over there." He pointed toward the temple before lowering his hand to re-tie the *tilmantli* on his right shoulder, the white cloak that draped to cover his arms.

Tia gave a nod and scurried the direction he indicated. A crowd still gathered around the painting which was propped against the stairs. She took a step closer, hoping to have her turn. At last, an old woman moved away, allowing Tia to look at the depiction of several men. *White.* Never had she seen skin of the fairness of the group in the painting, and the figure so prominent at the front? A white man whose serene face seemed to speak to her. He was obviously the leader. A sharp point arose from his head, the material matching his breastplate. The lower half of his face was covered with a dark, bristled hair. His chocolate eyes peered from beneath bushy brows. The rest of his face was pale, like a shaft of flax, nothing like the shade of her own copper color.

Fair skin. White. Not impossible after all.

If this man were truly the one who had arrived upon the shores of Mejico, perhaps the great white god really had arrived and the stories were true. She wanted even more to see her parents, to let them know that she too now believed.

17

The small strip of land before them was not their final destination. Felipe had already heard Cortés discuss who would accompany him on an inland march, following the quest gold. All three massive ships were anchored near the shore. Four crewmen lowered a sloop from the side of the supply freighter then rowed to the ship where Felipe stood.

"Sir, the ramp is ready for you to disembark," Miguel said. He stood at the rail where the plank had been lowered, leading from the ship to the smaller transport.

Several crew members held the bridge it formed steady. A cluster of men gathered behind the captain as he stepped into the sloop. Felipe counted twenty men—officers, the king's accountant, and Father Olmedo among them—who joined their captain. They would be the first to touch new soil. A flash of jealousy rushed through him. *Why should I feel this way? All those months ago, I thought I should never see a new land, as much as I wanted to. And, now, here I am, ready to go ashore.* He shook his head in amazement at his impatience.

Like the other men, Felipe stayed at his post on deck, watching the sloop carry his captain toward the natives standing along the beach. He noticed César standing at the opposite railing, also watching. Felipe could read the expression on his face. *Desire.* His enemy was not so different from himself after all. A silent truce had been reached between the two of them it seemed. Felipe avoided César, and César avoided him.

Three previous times the expedition had stopped at places along the coast, meeting with natives and receiving gifts. Cortés had always sent them away with a message: "Tell your leader I am coming." They had rushed from the deck, nearly falling into the water in their haste to disembark. Felipe's hopes for the journey to be nearly at its end were dashed when Cortés had again ordered the anchors raised and the ships to move out.

This encounter would be no different. Turning his gaze back toward the ship bearing Cortés, Felipe watched the meeting. The broad-shouldered man Felipe assumed was the leader of the group wore a breechcloth, and his chest was decorated with a heavy-looking beaded vest. His headdress was made of many-colored feathers and trailed down his back toward the ground, much longer than those of the others with him.

Each man bowed then Cortés offered gifts. Was this man different from the others who Cortés had mistreated? The native accepted the offering and brought out his own gifts. A lengthy conversation ensued, with the leaders walking along the shoreline, discussing as much through gestures as with words. Felipe wished he could hear what both Spaniard and native said. Of course, he would not have been able to understand the native anyway. If only the young woman from the ship had been with him. The conversations with each native group had seemed to introduce Cortés to their language, as well as their customs. This meeting appeared cordial.

Felipe allowed his attention to shift to the dissatisfaction he heard brewing among the crew. Was César among the men talking mutiny against Cortés because of his decisions concerning this expedition? Was he loyal to Velasquez, the Cuban leader, who Cortés had rushed to escape? Surely César would not be among those prepared to force Cortés into their immediate return now that their journey was proving fruitful. Didn't he covet this opportunity? Felipe would not abandon it before he stood upon the land, gathering riches before returning to Cuba.

And Manuela. He wanted to take riches for his raven-haired beauty who surely still awaited his return. His gaze sought out Cortés. The men had left the beach, and the sloop headed toward the main ships. The meeting with the natives must be finished.

Felipe moved to help draw the cords that would once again lift the plank into place. Although not sure if he trusted Cortés, at least the man had previous experience with native peoples. None of the other crew could say as much. Felipe would follow the Spaniard until Cortés proved himself unworthy of obedience.

The sloop pulled alongside, and the landing party rejoined the main crew topside.

"Gentlemen, I must tell you of the fierce battle that

rages between the leaders of this land," Cortés said almost as soon as he arrived.

Felipe stepped closer, wanting to hear everything Cortés discussed.

"These people are called *Totonac*. The *Cacique*, their leader, has offered an assembly of men to protect us against the warriors of Moctezuma, the leader of a people known as *Mejicas*."

Moctezuma. Felipe remembered the name from the lips of the woman who translated for the natives. *Totonac. Mejicas*. Felipe whispered the strange words, feeling their texture on his tongue. *Perhaps knowing the words will one day become useful,* he thought. If nothing else, he would use them to impress Manuela when he returned home.

"According to Malinche, the woman translator, they desire nothing more than to battle this evil leader," Cortés continued. "Malinche says the *Cacique* seeks allies."

"How do they feel about us?" one of the crewmen called, worry evident in his voice.

"They have already heard of us from the others we have encountered. They do not fear us because they feel no one can do more harm than Moctezuma," Cortés responded. "With us, they hope they will be able to overcome his power. If we join with the battle, the Mejicas' riches will become our riches, as the Totonacs only desire their land and Moctezuma's demise."

What sort of man must this Moctezuma be? Felipe wondered. *Will Cortés endanger us for his gold?*

"We will call this place *Villa Rica*–rich village, because it

97

will bring us much gold," Cortés continued. AA company of men from our second ship will be left behind to prepare a place for refuge should we experience trouble in our exploration or eventual battle with this Moctezuma."

Eventual battle? Felipe shuddered. *A battle might mean my death.*

18

Manuela counted the coins which Eduardo had brought today, eight pieces of copper. Added to her previous earnings, they made twenty-six. She wrapped them into the center of a finely-embroidered handkerchief her mother had made. The cloth and its contents were both precious to Manuela. One represented love, the other added freedom.

She tucked the package under the garments in her drawer then rose from the bed. Her long legs poked from beneath the hem of her skirt more each day. She was growing tall, and it was time for her to add a ruffle, preserving the skirt for another season of wear. But Manuela did not have time to care about her own clothing, choosing instead to spend her time stitching handkerchiefs to sell. Eduardo had sold the last piece today. To earn more money, she must work quickly to make more handkerchiefs.

"And I must have money," Manuela said, chastising herself for even taking the time to count what she already earned. She should have been able to calculate the total in her head, but she found she loved the touch of the coins against her palm.

Her father had finally told what he paid for her dowry—ten pieces of silver. Her copper coins might take years to equal even one piece. At first she had been discouraged but then grew determined. Manuela not only ran her papa's house, but she was also a working woman. She would repay him, while fulfilling all of her other obligations to him as well.

"Felipe . . ." Manuela sighed, glancing out her window toward the harbor. Her loneliness for him was no longer overwhelming, but great just the same. His continued absence forced her to mature in a way his presence might have taken a lifetime to achieve. Her earnings, though still small, gave her a sense of power over her fate. Conquering her fears helped her know she could wait, even if his return took her lifetime.

The sun dipped low, and bright rays of red streaked the sky. "Red sky at night," Manuela said, allowing the remaining prophesy to finish in her heart. *It will be fair weather, for the sky is red.*

She gathered the linen fabric and embroidery threads then moved closer to her regular sewing spot for yet another night, stitching the intricate patterns the women were apt to buy—tonight, the pattern of a ship upon the waters. She selected a brown thread and began to work, candlelight flickering shadows against the walls around her.

19

A flurry of activity began topside when the ship's anchor was dropped. Felipe found Miguel and the two of them pulled rope, lowering the plank which would allow Cortés to disembark for the second time. Felipe was uncertain how many men Cortés would allow to leave the ships this time.

A gathering of natives stood along the shoreline. The copper-skinned men were naked except for breechcloths and feathered necklaces. Were they friendly? They appeared to be holding gifts, welcoming the ships and their men to these shores, yet Felipe could not be sure. Appearances were not always what they seemed. Even the most respected lad could be evil inside. César was proof of that.

Cortés held the black flag, his standard, waving in the ocean breeze. His advisors gathered in a semi-circle behind him as Felipe and the others finished their task, the wooded plank making a splash when it touched the shallow waters a few feet from the white sand.

Felipe stepped back from the railing. All was silent as Cortés and his men gazed at the natives, trying to gauge their intentions. César had joined the men on deck. For these many months, Felipe had been successful at staying out of his dangerous reach, each of them assigned to a different part of the ship. Only at meal times had he caught a glance of the once-swaggering youth. Perhaps César had changed in the time that had passed, his boldness gone under the commands of the foreman.

But perhaps not. Felipe was surprised to see César move directly behind the expedition leader and his men. *Does he believe he will be among the first to stand on the soil of this land?*

"I bring you greetings from the king and queen of Spain." Cortés's voice boomed across the helm of the ship as he raised his hand in a sign of peace.

A rustle of whispers spread through the gathering of men below before they dropped to the ground, bowing their heads against the sand. A rhythmic murmur came from them as one voice. A chant.

Felipe tried to mimic the word, the thick accent making each sound difficult to decipher. "Quet . . . Quez . . . co . . . ahh . . . tall. Quetzalcoatl." He had heard the word twice now before. Still not a word he understood, but it seemed significant to those lying prone before the ship.

Cortés drew to his full height, jutting his breastplate forward as he looked at the men standing around him. "Gentlemen, these men recognize our greatness. We are as gods."

The conquistador began to descend to meet the natives. Felipe stayed on the ship, along with most of the sailors. César moved toward the plank as if planning to follow, but the others crowded him from the opening in their desire to watch Cortés. Felipe paid attention as Cortés greeted the leader. A chief, perhaps?

Father Olmedo, the Catholic priest who had traveled with them from Cuba, gave a brief message, a form of mass.

Cortés shouted, "I declare this land New Spain, *Neufue Espaigne.*" Gifts exchanged hands, delivered by a bevy of women—fourteen by Felipe's count—who offered their arms filled gold and jewelry.

Cortés had brought glass. Nothing of real value, at least not to the Spaniard or his men.

"Transparent. As is his purpose in being upon this land," Felipe whispered.

Are my reasons for being here just as clear? Like the gifts Cortés has brought, are my dreams also breakable?

20

Tia and Rebekha stood at the archway of the palace garden, looking toward the temple of Huitzilopochtli. The sky glowed orange just briefly, then blackened as smoke clouds blocked the daylight. Tia recognized the meaning, more sacrifices had been made and the bodies burned.

"Do you suppose it's another sign?" Rebekha twisted the fabric at the waistline of her tunic as she spoke. "Why should there be yet more prophesy when the great white god has already arrived upon our land?"

"Only a sign of Moctezuma, who has ordered more sacrifices at the temple," Tia said, a calm assurance in her voice. "Come." She reached to take the younger girl's hand, but Rebekha refused to give it.

"No. No." Rebekha shook her head and stepped farther away from the gate. "Quetzalcoatl may strike me dead if I draw too near."

"If Moctezuma doesn't deliver the blow first." Tia took a step beyond the archway. "I must see for myself whether god or man has brought us reason for this display of power."

"Tia, you can't go." Rebekha leaned toward her as

though she wanted to reach out and touch her friend, but her feet were rooted into place. "Please."

"I will return soon," Tia said as she started down the familiar path toward the market and the temple.

The closer she came, the more people had joined her direction, drawn to the fire like moths. By the time she reached the first market cart, the stench assaulted her nose, bringing tears to her eyes. Yet she walked on, unable to stop herself from viewing carnage she was certain she would find. Past experience had taught her what happened on the top of the temple, and this time would be no different, she was certain. Yet the thought still passed into her mind: What god would demand the slaughter of so many to protect an unrighteous ruler such as Moctezuma?

The *zólaco* was filled with people both nobles and slaves intermixed at the base of the temple. Flames shot into the sky from its apex. The smell of fire mingled with the acrid odor of scorched flesh. Guards stood at the steps, spears readied to prevent anyone from trying to ascend the stairs to stop the ruler's efforts to satisfy the jealous white god.

Tia worked her way just close enough to the throng to hear Moctezuma's shouted words. "Oh great Huitzilopochtli, we are ever grateful for this land which you gave unto our ancestors. We know you have the power to protect us from intruders who wish to remove us from our holy purpose."

A few steps from the crowd, near the token of the moon goddess Coyolxauhqui, Queen Aramonia and Moctezuma's other wives stood as honored guests. The queen's face was lifted upward toward her husband, a sign of worship. *But worship* for *Huitzilopochitli, Quetzalcoatl,* or *Moctezuma himself?* Tia wondered.

Moctezuma continued, "We sacrifice this day in your honor, to prove worthiness of your continued blessings." The flames sent ash high into the air, punctuating his next words. The lifeblood of those who serve you stands as a promise of our continued trust in your desire to have us rule this land."

"*Us* meaning *you,* Moctezuma," she whispered. Her eyes were riveted onto the scene being played out above her. The rhythmic chanting of *Quet-zal-co-atl* from the voices of hundreds of Mejicas beat against her eardrums and flowed into her chest.

At Moctezuma's signal, a set of guards brought another prisoner—an elderly man—to the temple apex, likely not daring to dissent and become the next sacrificed. They held his wrists when his body tugged, trying unsuccessfully to writhe free from their grips, too old and frail to fight the guard. Screams pierced the air as the black-hooded priest shoved a knife into the old man's stomach then pulled the blade high into his chest. He withdrew the knife and shoved his hand into the cavity, drawing forth the still-beating heart and ripped it loose. The old man's screams stopped and his body fell lifeless to the stone altar.

The priest held the heart high above the temple, his cloak rustling in the breeze. A living river of blood coursed down his arm and onto the stone steps, blending with the permanent stains of so many previous sacrifices. When the blood stopped, the priest chopped off the old man's arms and legs and tossed them, along with his body, onto the pyre before the next victim was brought.

Tia fought the bile that rose to her throat. *Could any god be this cruel?* Certainly not the god Malinche said her parents now worshiped. An overwhelming rush of desire to meet that white god coursed through her, yet she sensed this temple was not where she would find him. She turned, weaving her way once again toward home. As much as the supreme leader prayed it would not be so, the white god would come into the very heart of the palace. Moctezuma's fear would draw him.

She wanted to be there to see this bearded man, whose face she had seen only in a painting, if only to decide he was not the great white god. Not Quetzalcoatl.

21

"Who pounds so insistently upon my door?" Manuela placed the needle into her fabric as she scurried toward the ornamental *guanacaste* wooden door.

"Quick, Manuela. It is I, Eduardo. The ships have come. The ships have come."

Manuela threw open the door, letting her stitchery fall to the cobbled stones beneath her. She grabbed the boy by his shoulders and shook him. "What did you say? Felipe's ship? Cortés has returned?"

Eduardo wiped the sweat from his brow and took a deep breath. His tunic and sandals were covered with dirt. "It is too soon to tell for certain. They are still far from the shore. But there are three great vessels, like those of Cortés. Tall masts, with the flag of Spain. One man at the docks was speculating . . ."

"No time for more words," Manuela said as she let go of Eduardo and grabbed her shawl from its peg on the wall. "I must see for myself." She began to run, her sandals making little puffs of dust in front of Eduardo as he worked to keep up, tired already from his previous trip to her house from the docks. Only once did Manuela look back to see if he was following.

"Go on. I will catch you," Eduardo said, his breath struggling to add volume to his voice. He waved her on with a motion of his hand. She did not need a second gesture of encouragement.

When she entered, the familiar dock area was filled with dock crew. The salty air smelled of the sweat that poured from their backs as they worked. Her feet pounded against the wooden wharf as she headed straight to the slip where Cortés had departed over a year ago. No ship neared the mooring. Manuela held her hand against her forehead, trying to shade the blazing mid-day sun from her eyes. There, against the horizon she saw them. One. Two. Three ships, still tiny specks to the naked eye, but she was sure they would be more distinguishable through the lens of a telescope, if only she had one. Hadn't Eduardo said the vessels were of the same size as those Cortés had sailed?

"Manuela." Caught up, Eduardo moved toward her, dodging workers along the way. "Manuela," he called again as he drew nearer.

She turned and flung her arm in the direction of the vessels. "Are those the ones?"

His head bobbed an answer as he fought for breath to continue. "With as slow as they are progressing, they are at least . . . at least a day's sail yet . . . away . . . from shore."

"A day?" Manuela's voice was wistful, almost haunting in timbre. "I have waited many days for Felipe to return. I suppose I can wait one more."

As the hours wore on, the three ships grew larger against the horizon. Manuela knew ships came and went each day, with the workers only responding once the vessel was ready to dock, so she was not surprised that men on the wharf continued their business without caring that the vessels moved closer.

But not close enough for Manuela. "If only the winds were turned so I might see the flags. Eduardo, would you recognize the insignia of Cortés's fleet? I'm not sure I can yet see them." She bounced on the balls of her feet, trying to get a better position to look across the heads of the workers.

Eduardo said in the tone of a student reciting from memory, "The Royal Standard of Spain, an eagle atop a crest, with a yoke and arrow, the personal badges of King Ferdinand and Queen Isabella."

Her voice carried disappointment. "Oh. Nothing unique that might distinguish his ships from any others from the motherland?"

Eduardo shook his head. "Cargo ships never arrive in sets of three, only expeditions."

"Never?" Glancing toward the three ships across the water and praying Eduardo was right, she touched her hand against his sleeve and peered deep into his eyes, searching for the truth.

"Well . . . hardly ever," he amended. "It nears midday. There is still time before the ships arrive." Eduardo's stomach growled, as if agreeing with the message he hoped to convey.

Manuela giggled at the sound. "A hint that it is time to

eat?" She glanced again toward the water, noting the ships had only moved a hair's breadth closer. A heavy sigh rose from deep within her. "I suppose a brief respite would be good, and perhaps a solid meal will calm my heart."

"And my stomach," Eduardo said as he patted his belly.

Manuela smiled, shaking her head at his skinny frame. "If we don't feed you soon, you will waste away to nothing." As much as she hated to be away too long or gone too far, she asked, "Should we return to my house?"

"Mine is closer." Eduardo turned and headed toward the piazza, his hunger dictating the speed he moved down the dock. "There will be fresh fruit and *hutias*, the same kind of meat the explorer Christopher Colón ate on Christmas Day."

"I will eat as the explorers do," she said, a lightness in her voice that had been gone since Felipe disappeared, as she hurried along behind Eduardo. "There is only one thing that bothers me." She glanced once more toward the ships and allowed herself again to count them. One, two, three.

"And what is that?" Eduardo asked, waiting for her to catch up.

"Three ships," she said. "Didn't Cortés have other vessels to carry supplies and food?"

"Three masted *carracks* and eight brigantines." He looked again toward the ships, counting them aloud as though the importance of her question had struck him. "One, two, three . . . and no others. Manuela, you cannot give up hope. Let's wait and see. These ships may have traveled faster, or perhaps he gave up the others when the supplies were depleted."

"Or it is not Cortés, nor Felipe returning triumphant?" The flame of hope she had held in her heart at the arrival of three ships was snuffed out again by her own doubts.

22

A thrill went through Felipe as he took his first step on land, this land of the Mejicas. His body continued to feel the sway of the water that had long been beneath him. Like many of the others, Felipe sank to his knees and ran the warm golden grains of sand through his fingers.

"A fool and his treasure . . ." César stood above him, his eyes blazing as he looked toward Felipe, as though all the pent-up hatred had focused into their center. "This is all the gold you will touch on the journey."

"It is more than you will enjoy," Felipe said as he rose to his feet. A shove sent him sprawling in the loose sand. César's foot placed against Felipe's chest held him down, but he used his arm to wipe the sand from his mouth. Renewed hatred seethed within him as well. He had almost forgotten the way he felt toward César in the complacency that had come with months of no interaction.

"Riches or none, I will return to take the hand of Manuela," César said, his voice more the threatening tone he had used in Cuba. Not at all like the simpering child he'd become under the hand of the ship foreman. "You will be lucky to return. Sorry you will miss the wedding celebration."

Felipe shoved César's foot from his chest then jumped to his feet. "Bastard," he yelled as he delivered a shove of his own that took César off guard, knocking him into a heap. "What satisfaction would it give you to marry a girl whose passion for you is *hatred?*"

César scrambled to stand. "It will give me great satisfaction to turn her loathing toward *you.*"

He swung his right fist, but Felipe deflected the blow. Rage burst from César's entire body as he became a whirling dervish, intent on destroying his enemy. His fists pounded against Felipe's arms and face. Felipe countered, delivering a right hook to César's eye. He ignored the shouts from the crew, delivering a powerful blow to César's left rib while kicking his ankle, causing him to buckle for a moment. Felipe took advantage and smashed him in the nose.

Blood poured down César's face like an unbridled current. He made no attempt to curb the flow before speaking. "This is not over, you brazen prick."

A dozen members of the crew had gathered around Felipe. None stood near his opponent. He squared his shoulders, gathering his breath and focusing entirely on the bleeding enemy before him, spitting out the words, "And it won't be until you are dead and Manuela is in my arms."

"Gentlemen, save your anger."

Cortés. Felipe had not seen their captain join them.

"Anger will serve you well in the days of coming battle." The leader turned to address his men. "On to Chiahuitztla."

Beyond the circle, hundreds of natives waited, their backs loaded with woven baskets. Cortés raised his sword, and his own men fell into formation to march along the shore behind him.

César held a thumb and finger against his nose, pinching just below the bridge. He drew the other hands across his tunic, leaving red stains on the fabric. "We will see who is still alive once this is truly over." He gave another piercing look at Felipe before joining the last of the ranks following Cortés.

Alone for the moment, Felipe dropped once again to his knees, but he paid no attention to the golden sands. "Beloved Mary, protect me from the evil desires of these men. Forgive me for my own transgressions." His voice was nothing more than a whisper. "If it be the will of thy Son, the Holy Lord, deliver me safely home, back to Cuba and the loving arms of my dear, sweet Manuela." A sob choked from his throat. He gulped in air, trying to hold back the tears brimming within his eyes. At last, with the natives also filed away, Felipe ran to catch up with his crewmen.

23

Three days later, the Spanish efforts to help the Totonac battle against other tribes continued. None of the men had rested since the fighting began, with Cortés's push forward along the coast, his lust for gold over-weighing his concern for the welfare of his men. Felipe feared for his life not only because of César's threats, but also from his leader's single-minded drive to conquer Moctezuma.

Warriors not wearing the markings of the Totonac were cut down like cane in the fields. Felipe tried to stay back, away from the battlefront. He watched shipmates fall, blood pouring from open wounds. Bile rose within his stomach until it disgorged. Sweat formed above his brow, and he felt faint for a brief moment, but he marched on, following the battle. The fear of his leader served as motivation, not a desire to wipe out the tribes they encountered along the way. Where was the hero he thought Cortés was? There was nothing heroic in the mass slaughter of hundreds of men in the search for gold, just as Felipe felt no heroics in his own participation in this brutal war. He was not at all the victor he had seen himself to be in his childhood games.

At last the fighting calmed when the Totonac leader identified five native men, hiding in the nearby woods, as Moctezuma's tribute collectors, servants of the man they most wanted killed.

"Imprison these men," Cortés ordered. "Let Moctezuma stew about our plans for a few days. When we are prepared again for battle, his men will return with our message of respect for their king."

"It is done," the Totonac *cacique* said.

Cortés was smart enough to know that brute force might take down the general masses, but to overthrow their leader and discover the secret coffers of gold would require ingratiating himself to Moctezuma. Word had come through the ranks that the Mejicas leader thought Cortés to be the great white god he both worshiped and feared, the name the Totonacs had chanted when Cortés first stepped upon their land. *Quetzalcoatl*–that strange-sounding name again.

Cortés stopped the march along the coastline, the massacre of natives finished now that the goal of sending a message to Moctezuma was met. Relief flooded through Felipe. Already nearby tribes had sent men to join the Spaniard's forces against the Mejicas ruler. Surely Moctezuma would fear retaliation of his god if any more white men were lost in future battles.

Felipe joined the other exhausted shipmen sitting on the sandy beach, no longer golden, but soaked with blood.

One of the crew said to Cortés, "These tribute collectors say Moctezuma has sent you gifts and wishes to welcome you at his palace."

"Oh, he will," Cortés said, a smile upon his face, "and then the palace will be mine."

Although Felipe's leader's words did not hold promise of a peaceful settlement, or the possibility of negotiation, he hoped it was only a matter of time before Cortés had his riches, and the crew would be ordered back on the ships for their return to Cuba and glory. Claiming to want only the preservation of the cities and land as the foundation of a lasting colony, why did Cortés seem so bent to destroy everything in his path?

"Sink the ships," Cortés ordered. "All except the flag ship."

His voice was forceful, not one to be disobeyed, yet Felipe could hardly believe the words he had just heard. *Sink the ships?* The air whooshed from his lungs. *Surely Cortés has gone mad. We can't follow such orders!* But, men rushed forward to scuttle the supply ships, emptying the holds of the remaining barrels and crates, before pitching torches onto their upper decks. A cold sensation washed from Felipe's face through his entire body.

"We are here to conquer. We will prevail," Cortés shouted. "When we return to Cuba, it will be as one."

Sweet Mary, Mother of Jesus, what has Cortés done? Felipe fought the panic rising within him. *What will become of us?* His heart raced, sucking all of the air from his lungs. His last thought before darkness hit him was, *Will Maneula and I ever be one?*

When Felipe awoke, flames leaped from the deck, racing up the mast ropes on the ships. Had he witnessed the sight upon his return to Cuba, he would have considered the fires a victory celebration. But in this new world, fear gripped his heart, telling him the burning vessels were his death sentence.

He stood at the edge between sand and forest, watching. The warm summer day intensified like the heat of a funeral pyre. He longed for a drink from the water casks lining the shore, but his feet would not move toward the burning mass. A flood of rats swarmed the beach, escaping from the heat that overwhelmed their months-long home. The creatures surged amid the hundreds of men armed with crossbows, standing beside cannons. Weapons were useless against both the rodents and the flames.

As the smoke rolled past him, Felipe heard the whinny of several horses in the woods behind him where they had been tethered earlier. Cortés stood watching the flames. Next to him a man Felipe recognized from the portraits he had seen in Cuba, a man long counted dead. Jéronimo de Aguilar, a Spaniard who joined them as part of the Totonic tribe, who had been gone from the homeland for eight years, was now at last returned to his countrymen. Had he been held hostage by these natives? No Spanish ship other than those of Cortés had been in the harbor. Perhaps his own ship had sunk, leaving him stranded here with these people. The stories Felipe had heard while still in Cuba revered this man as having been sacrificed for the good of their homeland.

Moving closer to the two men, curious as to what Cortés intended to do now that his ships were gone, Felipe could hear what the Spaniard said.

"We should call this the Island of Sacrifices."

Does the man read my mind? None of the others standing around Cortés seemed to respond. Their silence rang in Felipe's ears louder than the ocean. Even the scores of natives stood in awe at the display upon the waters. *Sacrifices.* Felipe had seen enough lives sacrificed. He had seen enough of this land. His curiosity was satisfied. He wanted more than anything to board the remaining ship and sail away. Away from the land of Moctezuma. Away from his own ruthless leader.

"We should have overtaken him while still at sea, before we lost so much." César spoke into Felipe's ear like a friend, a confidant.

Startled, Felipe looked into the eyes of his enemy. "*We?* I am not part of your conspiracy to overtake this expedition."

"Can't a friend make an offer, especially one that might save your life?"

"Friend?" Felipe could hardly stifle the laugh that came from deep within him. "I thought you wanted to see me dead."

"Perhaps we can settle our disputation in the manner of men," César said, placing his hand on Felipe's shoulder, a gesture men often used to forward a negotiation. Immediately it was shrugged off, but César continued. "I will still win Manuela's heart, but our mutiny needs a crew if it wishes to sail the remaining ship back to Cuba."

Felipe looked toward the conquistador, who was speaking to the masses. Most of them seemed to be listening with rapt attention, bursts of applause punctuating their approval of the Spaniard's words. Did he still believe in Cortés's judgment and ability to take them safely home? Already so many men were lost, and the promise of continued battle did not calm his fears.

Cortés's voice carried as Felipe listened. "In the morning, we press on, carrying out the wishes of God." Another round of cheers erupted from the crew and natives.

Whose god? He looked back at César. *Do I face the dangers before us at the side of Cortés, or should I join with he who wants me dead?*

"Are you with us, or will your loyalties remain with the man who denies you the means to return to Cuba?"

César stood, hands upon his hips—a sign of patience, or defiance? Felipe wasn't sure. But there was one thing he was certain of, his best chance of survival still lay with the captain. "I have made my decision," he said, then quickly moved through the crowd to stand beneath the standard positioned near Cortés. The golden words fluttered above his head: *If we have faith, we shall conquer.*

24

The sun crested then began its descent into the western sky, yet Manuela continued to wait at the docks. Eduardo had placed a chunk of bread, a ripe grapefruit, and dried pork into a pouch for her, knowing he would never pull her away from the seaside a second time. She carried a skin of fresh water as she had left Eduardo's house, prepared to sit at the docks and watch the tiny specks on the horizon grow into ships.

"I will join you later, after I've finished my work and dined with my mother," her friend promised.

"There is no hurry," Manuela assured him. "You said yourself the fleet would take a full day to arrive, and that time has not yet passed."

"True, although their colors will be proven before they dock."

She nodded. "But the flag alone does not give the identity of which sailors are on board."

The hot, humid air bathed her skin which had begun earlier to tingle under the sun's rays. Her lower back ached from constantly stretching, hoping to catch a better glimpse and identify the flag that was still too far away. Her eyelids grew heavy with the tedium of the task. She fought to stay awake, as if one lost moment of vigilance would curse the banners, changing them from those of her motherland into the standard of an enemy nation.

The ships had moved close enough now to have definite outlines. The white masts billowed, filled with the same breeze Manuela could feel against her face. "Faster," she whispered. "Bring Felipe home to me."

A rush of memories flooded her heart. Afternoons spent on this very shore with Felipe, listening to his dreams of sailing with an explorer, discovering new worlds. She recalled that even as a small boy, his games centered in the love of the sea. Every outcropping of rock became a deck where he would stand, legs braced against the rolling of the waters, commander of an imaginary vessel. Eduardo, Miguel, and his other friends gathered around him, mates dedicated to the success of each voyage.

In the village streets, Felipe and his hearty crew fought wicked pirates under the command of the evil César, who was not aware of this charade being played out at his expense. The early loss of his father had taken all sense of fun from him even then. He saw the other boys only as a threat to his power. Hatred had already grown in his heart for Felipe, evidenced in the way he spoke, spitting each word from his mouth like melon seeds. He always stood erect, carriage dignified beyond his years. His eyes betrayed burning feelings of anger from deep within his soul.

Except when they looked upon Manuela. At first she

had been unable to read the hidden messages. She had stood aside, the dutiful maiden who waited the return of her explorer, as the boys carried out their elaborate childhood drama. César's attention had only irritated her. Then as they grew older, it became uncomfortable, and his gaze grew bolder. What would he do to Felipe as they sailed the great ocean with Cortés? What had he already done? She battled the constant burn of worry for his safety.

She had known the moment Felipe read the bulletin that day he would find a way to board Cortés's ship, ready to sail away. Her relief that he was not chosen was enormous, even as his pain must have been. She didn't know how he had managed to, but Manuela never doubted that Felipe was living his dream, sailing the ocean, discovering new worlds, meeting new cultures, as Colón had done. Had she realized as a child the loneliness she would feel at Felipe's departure, she would have tried to steer him away from this place. She would have begged him to stay. Pleaded harder. No, her heart told her the truth. She would not have tried to stop him. To do so would have taken away the very core of his existence, the love of adventure that had first drawn her to him. She could not ask him to be something he was not. So she was destined to wait—forever, if that's what it took.

The supper hour passed with her food from Eduardo untouched. The flag ship had pulled ahead some time ago, and Manuela could see the crest. Disappointment washed over her heart. The colors were wrong—the green stripe belonging to Italy instead of Spain—and there was no eagle. The banner did not belong to Cortés, but she could not walk away.

She felt a gentle hand cup her elbow. Eduardo had come. They stood in silence as the ship made its final approach to the docks. Workers scurried around them, grabbing lead ropes tossed from the deck, shouting as they guided the massive vessel into the slip, then tied it down.

As the men worked Manuela strained to understand the conversation, much of it in a language other than her own. At first only single words floated toward her. *Velasquez. Trinidad. de Aguilar.* Still she waited, piecing together bits of information until at last she worked out the truth. Although these ships did not sail under Cortés, the men surely knew of him. They were being sent under the direction of Governor Velasquez in a second expedition to follow the path of the lost explorer Jéronimo de Aguilar, the same direction Cortés had taken. Once supplies were garnered and the ship's holds refilled, they would again set sail.

Would they find the man believed long dead, the lost explorer de Aguilar? Would they overtake Cortés and claim the riches he sought for Velasquez instead of King Ferdinand as was his goal? Would these men and their new ships not only find Cortés, but also escort his ships back to Cuba, bringing Felipe with them? The flame of hope that had extinguished within Manuela earlier in the day began to take on new life, a tiny flicker. Compared to the years since Cortés had first begun his journey from Spain, the time he been gone from Cuba likely seemed minuscule to these men, but to her the year he and been gone seemed forever.

Dark settled as Manuela and Eduardo approached the dock workers, finding one who seemed to be in charge.

Manuela asked, "Kind sir, once this ship sails, how long might it be before we expect it to return?"

The man merely glanced at them before offering his gruff reply. "Two years at the least, more likely three. Longer if they encounter that devil Cortés and fight to gain the riches he has claimed."

Manuela stepped back, her hand fluttering to her chest. Might Felipe be gone another year or more before she hoped to see him? As she took in the enormity of his answer, she wondered why she had never asked this very question before. Or had she simply refused to listen, believing her beloved would return swiftly? Tears welled up in her eyes as Eduardo again took her elbow and led her away from the docks.

25

By listening to the men Cortés entrusted as senior captains, Felipe learned the Spanish were assured passage through the republic, but instead the armies encountered a hostile force and engaged in two battles alongside the Totonic people against the Tlascalans. Cristóbal de Olid, one of the captains, had been wrong, and another twenty men or more were dead, a few Felipe knew by name.

He made sure he was away from the advance line, fearing for his own life. When he had played as a child at being an explorer, he had not anticipated violence would be the mainstay of the discovery of a new world. Yet Cortés seemed to draw battle and bloodshed to him.

The day before, he had sent Francisco de Córba and a party of twenty-five men to scout the region to the west. Word had come this morning they had been ambushed by the Tlascalan warriors. At dusk, the warriors withdrew into the forests, and Felipe feared many more of his crewmates would die now that Cortés had abandoned the shore, ready to forge his way inland toward Moctezuma's riches. Since de Córba's group had been ambushed, nothing would prevent the Tlascalans from a more bold move against the main forces of Cortés.

The captain had ordered several men to watch the camp as the others settled in to sleep. Felipe sank onto his mat, grateful night had descended. His body cried out for rest, but it took a long time for his mind to relax.

Awaking with a start, Felipe heard voices as others around him also stirred. He heard the clink of chain-mail. "What's happening?" he asked Miguel who lay near him.

"It sounds like we are regrouping for an attack," Miguel said. He stood and rubbed his eyes in an effort to fully awaken, then grabbed his own breastplate.

Felipe checked his belt for the dagger he kept stored in its sheath. Men rushed past him, forming ranks outside of the camp in preparation for the ensuing battle. Felipe's heart was torn. *I desired adventure, and now that it comes I want nothing more than home.*

"Hurry, Felipe," Miguel said, urging him to move into position.

Captain Gonzalo de Sandoval gave the call to arms. The cannon fire startled Felipe into movement. Each of their men had been given a musket and ammunition. Felipe touched the knife he wore at his waistband, hoping he would not be involved in combat close enough to use it. He must live to see Manuela again. Relief that he did not encounter any murderous natives on his way, he joined others from his crew already on the advance.

Hundreds of men rushed through the wooded area; some fell wounded, others dead. The battle was swift, yet harsh. Felipe winced at the signs of bloodshed, and the dead bodies that lay around him, most of them natives. *Could we be winning the battle?* Almost before it began, he heard the cry to cease fire. And not once had he encountered a living Tlascalan warrior.

He aided in the gathering of men, both dead and wounded, before their troops reassembled, not awaiting instructions from their leader. He found Miguel and worked with him on setting pyres for a proper burial ceremony.

"Their ambush failed," Miguel said, a smile upon his face.

Felipe did not feel like smiling. This battle would not be the last. His mind filled with rushing thoughts. *Will Cortés expect us to kill all those we meet along our journey, or will he be able to negotiate settlements along the way? Where are the Totonic who promised to stay at our side as we overtook the Mejicas leader, Moctezuma?* One more question pressed upon his mind, bringing him as much worry as any of the others. *How many men can we lose and still sail the ship we have left to our homeland, and will I be upon it?*

Captain Pedro de Alvarado issued a call to assemble then spoke to the men. Felipe and Miguel stopped the preparations they were making, and drew nearer to listen. "We have defeated the Tlascalans. They have agreed to let our army pass, and they will furnish any provisions we need. Prepare to march."

Miguel and Felipe looked first at each other, then toward the pyre and the bodies that had already been brought to the ship. An order was an order and they must obey, so they joined the ranks, marching a short distance to the Tlascalan capital. Once they arrived, Cortés ordered a cross erected at the site and a dozen or so men immediately got to work, while Father Olmedo offered a brief mass.

When the construction and mass were done, Cortés spoke, indicating the leaders of the Tlascalans, "Our friends, we desire only to march to the palace of Moctezuma. We wish your people no harm. Join us in our ensuing battle against the king, and the land of the Mejicas will be yours."

A cheer went up among those gathered in the city square, all except Felipe.

26

Each day Tia made sure she had time to go to the temple square. Today the conversations along the market plaza had been of the joined forces of Totonic, Tlascalan, and the strangers with their leader, Cortés. She learned this new name from the jade merchant who had just returned from the water where the sun rose.

"The sun fights darkness every night to rise each morning and save mankind," he said. "Moctezuma and the Mejicas people will prevail." His skin was wrinkled, and she thought his eyes seemed filled with wisdom, but she worried there might be no saving her people if his story was true.

She shifted her basket of maize, beans, and squash into her left hand.

"This man Cortés intends to come into Tenochtitlán to meet with Moctezuma," the merchant said. "Along the way, many warriors have been slain. The band even now marches through Cholula." He dug his hands into the box of gemstones set before him, letting them run like water through his fingers, then holding a few toward her on his opened palms for inspection.

"But are the Cholulans not our friends?" Tia asked, certain she had heard the palace elders speak kindly of this tribe. She picked up a small green gem and inspected it for cracks on the surface. Satisfied, she handed a copper coin to the merchant.

"They are indeed servants of our lord." He dropped the coin into the jeweled pocket of his robe. "They will offer men and kindnesses to bring the white god into Tentocholan without ire. Moctezuma believes if he greets his enemy with precious gifts, our land will not be conquered and the gods will bless us."

She remembered the words of prophesy. *He fears for his own safety if he does not welcome the white god.* If the prophesy was fulfilled, Moctezuma would send his closest advisors into the temple flames. But, she realized, not before he had sent hundreds of others.

"Aren't we all at risk?" The jade merchant echoed Tia's fears as though he had read her mind. A few women, slaves by their unadorned attire, moved closer to the merchant's cart. He again ran stones through his fingers, hoping to show the gems off in the best light.

She had to know for herself what these white men were like. Would she be able to discern by just looking at them if they were indeed the fulfillment of prophesy? She rolled the smooth jade she had purchased over and over in her palm as she made her decision, calling upon Chalchiuhtlicue, the goddess of springs, rivers, lakes, and the sea. A thought came into her soul in an instant, and she knew what she must do. "From which direction are they coming? How do I get there?"

He looked away from his new customers only briefly. "Follow the canal toward the morning sun. This is the causeway their men will follow across the water and into the center of our palace." He gave a single nod then offered a stone to the eldest of the women.

Tia passed through the city, the sun shimmering against the white buildings that lined her way. She had not explored this direction before. Lush green gardens surrounded the adobe homes as she neared the water. It was nothing like the river that passed through the city, its saltiness mixed with the wastes dumped from barges, giving off a strong odor. This water was devoid of aroma.

When at last she stood at the water's edge, she was struck by the beauty of the panorama before her. The sparkling blue of the water, the distant mountains capped with snow, the greenery of the mainland across the water's expanse. Her heart roared for home, not the palace where she lived, but the land of her birth. A strip of land wended its way all the way to the mainland. A catch came into her throat as she realized this lake which divided them might be crossed on foot.

"Oh, my mother," she said.

What if I were to leave? Her mind began to tick off the things she would need to take with her. Extra clothing. Food. A bedroll. *Would I need a weapon?* She knew she would.

133

Moctezuma's men could do anything to her if she were discovered.

"Cortés." She said the name aloud, testing her tongue against the strange new word.

The action made her think of her friend Malinche. *Will I ever see her again?* She doubted it if she left Tentochilan. But to leave the palace, running far away from the orders of Queen Aramonia, and escaping Moctezuma and his sacrifices seemed wonderful. The idea brought lightness to her thoughts that she hadn't allowed to grow before. Knowing escape might be possible gave her even more reason to live. She searched the path of the land bridge. Trees appeared to be moving closer to her as she watched. No. No, not the trees. Men. A large group of men. Were these the men she had so wanted to see? But she was not ready.

Now that the thought of leaving Tentochilan had entered her mind, the seed of truth grew in her heart. She must go. She must leave this city and its wicked leader before it was too late, before she became a sacrifice at the temple of his god. Turning, Tia began to run back the way she had come. There was much to prepare, and these white men might provide her the way to escape.

"Quetzalcóatl. Quetzalcóatl." The cry passed from the treetops where Moctezuma had long kept sentries in the trees to watch and report. Because Tenochtitlán was surrounded by shallow water, they were always vulnerable, including within their own nation. "Quetzalcóatl. Quetzalcóatl."

She had grown during the years she lived in Tenochtitlán. No longer a child, she wasn't afraid to think for herself. Why had she not thought of this plan before? She could take care of her own needs, protect herself from danger if necessary. She would meet the enemy before her and discover if he were white or Mejicas.

But not now. She must prepare to leave. The time for action had come.

27

The stack of completed handkerchiefs had grown to thirty, each a piece of art because of Manuela's dedication. Her collection of coins included many coppers but few pieces of silver. Eduardo had done well at selling her work, but he had been unable to sell even a single piece now for several weeks.

"So many women own your embroidery, I'm not sure who to sell to," he had said when he returned the selection last taken to the market. "And they only buy them one or two at a time."

Undaunted, Manuela cut the new bolt of pure white fabric into long strips instead of squares. Embroidery could embellish the ends of neck scarves as well as handkerchiefs. She set to her work immediately. As she stitched, she considered the finished pieces. Should she ask Eduardo to take them to the market in another city? No, he would be too shy to venture forth, dealing with people he didn't know. Perhaps she could modify the pattern, adding new colors, highlighting the delicate designs in some way. But that wouldn't make the women purchase more of the fine linens than they needed. At least Eduardo revealed the reasons why her work was no longer selling. This setback was something she could rectify, but she longed for a way to make a profit from the already finished pieces.

At dusk Papa came home with news. "I sold two cows to a merchant ship today. They are headed toward Spain and wish to have fresh milk aboard for their men."

"That's wonderful, Papa," Manuela said.

"Tonight I am a wealthy man. Let's celebrate before the truth that I still must sell more cows if I want to meet our needs in the coming winter hits me in the morning."

Manuela chuckled as she set her embroidery aside and moved toward the cupboard. "A cup of lime juice and a shared caimito?" She loved the purple star-shaped fruit which she sliced and arranged onto plates for the two of them.

He reached to take a plate from her. "These men have discovered that the foods and artistry of our land bring a good price among the Spanish people," Papa said. "They are interested in all sorts of products to sell once they return to the continent, making a profit on both ends of their journey."

Manuela glanced at the completed handkerchiefs on the nearby table. An idea struck her as her father talked. Would these wealthy merchants be interested in buying her wares to take to the homeland? Perhaps the women of Spain would find her work artistic. How much money could she get for the thirty completed pieces? Should she ask Eduardo to make the trade? Although he had done well at selling her work among the local women, would he strike a good deal with the men who were traders? Perhaps she could ask her father, but he knew nothing of the coins she had already collected toward repaying her dowry. He believed her work to be dedicated to the completion of finery for her own home once the chosen husband, César, returned.

Could she sell the handcrafted pieces herself? Her heart began to race. She would try. If she could not barter a fair sum, then she would ask Eduardo to approach the merchants for her. This could be the solution to her problem. If she could earn silver instead of copper for her work, she would reach her goal so much faster.

She chastised herself for not thinking of the trade ships before now. All these months she had gone to the docks, focusing only on the one thing she didn't see, the ships of Cortés returning with her Felipe onboard. Allowing her mind to dream of these new possibilities as her papa finished his fruit and retired, Manuela knew she would not be able to sleep.

She cleaned up after their repast and drew the curtain across her father's door. She would stay by the candle throughout the night, working on the scarf, the piece of embroidery she had just begun. This pattern would be special, one worthy of a queen. Perhaps Isabella herself would one day wear the work of a poor girl, hungry for the return of her beloved, one more valuable to her than all the riches in the world.

28

Cortés had taken no prisoners, but he had acquired an interpreter. He called her by the name *Malinche*, and Felipe actually met the girl when the men gathered to eat, picking bananas from the trees around them. He had seen her once before at a previous encounter with the natives. She was perhaps two years older than he was. Rumors said Cortés received her as a gift from the native chieftain, the *Cicique*.

As he ate, Felipe had a chance to look closely at the young woman. She wore an ankle-length skirt of flaxen fabric. Her blouse was tucked into a belt adorned with tiny gold and copper decorations. Malinche's feet were clad in leather sandals, but the skin seemed to be just as toughened and worn as the shoe. A series of looped bands held back her long, ebony hair. He wondered if he would have the chance to speak with her. Would Cortés allow his men to engage in such a conversation? Felipe had started to pick up a few words of the native tongue, and he yearned to use them with someone who might understand.

"Beautiful, isn't she?" The sound of César's voice

startled Felipe. "Perhaps this native will satisfy your desires when I return and take Manuela."

Felipe felt the fire of rage well within him. He looked directly into César's eyes then decided to strike back in another way than fighting as they had earlier done. "I thought you intended to return to Cuba before now. What happened to the mutiny?"

César placed his palm against Felipe's lips as he glanced around him. "Fool! Do not say the word so that others might hear."

Grabbing César's wrist, Felipe yanked the hand away then whispered, "Are you afraid there are too many against you?"

"Not so many that we cannot overcome." His voice changed to a deeper, threatening tone as he continued. "*You* have a greater enemy to worry about."

It was a small comfort to Felipe knowing that César had not done him any harm since the start of the voyage. The battling natives posed a greater threat—their clubs, spears, rocks, blowguns and bows with poisoned arrows could find their way past the heavy plate of armor Felipe wore on his chest. Their weapons might harm his body, but César's words were aimed at his mind. His knowledge of Manuela's love for him protected his heart.

"Prepare to march." Felipe recognized the voice as de Alvarado.

"We will continue this later," César said before slipping away into the ranks of men following orders.

Felipe took his own place in line. He could no longer

see where Malinche had been sitting and knew she would now be at Cortés's side in the front of the march.

The descent into the valley was a beautiful sight. Clear, sparkling water surrounded a massive island. Mountains edging the scene wore smoky skirts and white coverings of snow on their peaks. The sun poured over the land, warming the foliage and earth into a musky odor.

As Felipe moved closer to the bay, he realized they would enter the island by crossing a land bridge. A river of golden water issued from the capital. The dwellings sparkled in the brilliant sun, and one lone building in the center towered over the others.

This is a land of riches, Felipe thought. *A land of enchantment.*

29

The plaza around the palace swarmed with activity by the time Tia arrived, back from the causeway. Large numbers—merchants, peasants, slaves, and priests among them—pushed against the front wall, begging the guards to let them enter. The message she had heard her entire way became a chant as the people tried to force their way into Moctezuma's fortress.

"Quetzalcoatl! Quetzalcoatl! The great white god has come." The voices were high pitched, panic-filled.

Her head beat the message in a searing ache. She slipped through the secret back gates. The entrance-way known only to those who lived within the palace was too well-disguised for an intruder to notice. She entered the serene garden area, pausing only for a moment to regain her breath. Massaging her forehead, she wished for a better plan than just gathering her clothing and sleeping mat and trying to escape from the city and along the causeway to freedom.

Somehow she must meet one of the white men, ask him the right questions to test his leader's deity then decide if she would stay to worship or flee to the land of her birth. But how would she understand the words of a white man?

Inside the palace, the flurry of activity was nearly the same intensity as she had seen outside the gates. Staying close to the passage wall, she made her way toward her living quarters. No one paid attention to her as they rushed from place to place, carrying water jugs, heavy boxes, stacks of apparel, and prepared foods.

Surely these are not for the mob pressing against the gates, she thought. Moving into the great room which separated the slave quarters from those of the supreme ruler and his many wives, she leaned against the cool stone, listening to the chatter of those who moved around her. She caught only occasional words— "Thunder sticks . . . Giant dogs of war . . . Weapons never seen before."

At last she spotted Rebekha. Anxious to tell the girl what she had seen, she started to move across the room. A sudden hush and an open clearing brought her to a halt. All the others had fallen to their knees, bowing before the supreme ruler. For a brief moment, Tia looked directly into the eyes of Moctezuma, and she saw his fear. She had long known the great white god was a threat to the Mejicas leader. The moment of his trial was near as his own people rushed to the palace, needing his assurance that all was well. Soon the man believed to be Quetzalcoatl would also arrive. No wonder Moctezuma had sent so many to the temple since the messengers had first brought word of the ships.

Horror struck her mind. What was she doing? She dropped to the floor and lay prostrate before him. *Will he send me to the temple because of my boldness?* There was no other movement or sound. She held her breath as long as she could, then slowly let it out. Tears welled in her eyes as she thought of her mother and how she wanted to see her just one last time. She heard the chant outside increase in volume. "Quetzalcoatl! Quetzalcoatl!"

Moctezuma's fear could be heard in his voice. "How am I supposed to deal with this god?"

Tia looked up just enough to see the swish of his white robe and teal headdress feathers as he strode past her toward the palace doors. Relief washed through her body. Death had passed her by. She could not chance another meeting with Moctezuma if she were to fulfill her plan for escape.

"Tia, come." Rebekah stood at her side, pulling her to her feet. "Moctezuma has gone to stop the riot at the door. He is hungry for more sacrifices before the white god arrives." The two girls hurried into the passage toward the slave quarters. "You must hide or one of those sent may be you."

That is my very fear. She joined Rebekah, hurrying toward her room and praying she would find a way to get out of here.

30

The merchant ship stood at the dock as Manuela approached, her completed handkerchiefs wrapped in her shawl for protection. Only a few barrels dotted the boardwalk. A half-dozen men worked at loading the final casks onto the ship's deck. Her months of vigilant watching for Felipe's ship had taught Manuela that this vessel would soon embark. She must find the purchasing agent right away if she wanted to sell her wares.

"Pardon me," Manuela said to the burly sailor nearest her. "Is this ship departing for the motherland?"

The man's look at her was a leer, as though he had never seen a girl before. She wondered if indeed he hadn't, at least not for a very long time. His face was coarse, the lower half covered in bristles. Shaggy locks of matted hair hung against his shoulders. The odor emanating from him said he'd not bathed for longer than Manuela cared to know.

Perhaps he doesn't understand the language. She tried a simpler question— "Spain?"—as she gestured from the ship toward the ocean.

He gave her a curt nod before answering, "Yeah, this

one's headed there. Won't be taking a lass like you aboard, though, much as I'd like to." He moved his eyes up and down her body, coming to rest in the area just below her collarbone.

Manuela raised her hand to her breast, flustered by his response. "Oh, no. I . . . that's not my intention . . ." His gaze stayed riveted on her. She looked at the other men who were working to load another barrel onto the ship.

From above on the deck, she heard, "Don't mind him, Senorita. He lost his manners many years ago."

Manuela held a hand against her forehead so she could see past the morning sun. A uniformed man, much older, leaned against the main deck railing. He stared at her with a look of curiosity. Stepping away from the rude man on the dock, and looking up at the uniformed man, she said, "Perhaps you can help me."

"Anything for a beautiful woman."

Manuela felt the color rush into her cheeks. She had not thought of herself as a *woman*, let alone *beautiful*, but the realization that the passage of time had started to move her toward maturity hit her with his words. *Have I changed? Will Felipe recognize me when he returns?*

"What can I do to serve you?" The man had moved toward the gangplank and was descending onto the dock.

Taking a deep breath, she said, "I need to see the purchasing agent. Perhaps he would like to buy a product from me to take to Spain."

The first sailor guffawed before saying loud enough that Manuela could hear him, "I can think of plenty of things from you *I'd* like to take." The other men around him nodded as if they agreed.

"You're in luck." The uniformed man now stood beside her. "I am the agent for this vessel. Let's step into my office aboard ship and discuss the matter."

"Probably wants to do more than discuss, I'd say." The last barrel lifted onto the ship as the sailor tugged the pulley rope, his muscled arms straining with the effort.

For a fleeting second, Manuela wondered if Felipe's muscles were so well-developed. He was old enough for a beard to mask his face. *Will I recognize Felipe anymore quickly than he will recognize me?*

Manuela hoped the man was wrong about the officer's intentions. She wanted to earn money, but not in any way that would bring shame to herself. She clutched the shawl and handkerchiefs closer to her breast. The agent held out his arm, escorting her away from the crude sailor.

She stepped onto the plank, her heart pounding with each step she took toward the deck as an overwhelming rush of love for Felipe engulfed her. Boarding a ship such as this had been the fulfillment of his lifelong dream. Marrying Felipe would be hers.

31

Marching, marching, marching—Felipe crossed the sandy beaches, traversed through the wooded forest, and moved into hamlets where Moctezuma's emissaries offered generous bribes to get them to turn back—a golden eagle head, several bells, and a pendant resembling a rattlesnake tail, among others. The workmanship on the gifts was intricate. The Spaniard inspected each piece as it was given him then held his hand out to accept more. The gold only made him want more. It didn't stop his progress toward the city.

Malinche had identified Moctezuma's nephew, sent to welcome the Spaniards and their entourage of natives. He brought priests with him who performed tricks, hoping to use magic to frighten Cortés with their powers. Flashes of light, stones that came to life like turtles against the land, water that appeared to be blood red. Still Cortés marched his men on like a giant black serpent crossing the salty water toward the capital city of Tenochtitlan.

Felipe stood behind the gold-embroidered banners—*Comrades, with true faith follow the Holy Cross and through it we shall conquer.* The members of the ranks carried brass guns, crossbows, and steel swords. Four men pulled *falconets,* the cannon wheels making ruts as they moved through the trodden soil. Cortés, his senior captains, and a spattering of other men dressed in mail shirts, breast plates, leg armor, and steel *gorget* collars sat astride horses. Cortés carried his visored helmet in the crook of his arm. He wore a heavy gold chain around his neck with a single amethyst adorning his chest.

Felipe, as most of the men, had no such protection. The flaxen fabric of his tunic was marked with the soil of daily wear. He longed for a change of clothes, but they were too close to their destination now to turn back now.

As each man stepped onto the island, they gathered around the leader's horse, leaving enough room for him to dismount. Excitement coursed through Felipe as he found a spot not far from his captain. At last they were in the heart of this land. Cortés would soon meet with Moctezuma, more gifts would be exchanged, and their company would be back on the ship, returning to Cuba, he hoped. Cortés had begun his quest at the age of nineteen, nearly fifteen years ago. Felipe was grateful he had only been with him the past two years—two years of marching and fighting the natives—and he hoped their journey home would be less eventful than their time already on the continent.

Malinche stood at Cortés's side as he knelt, sword upright in the sand, and said, "I Hernán Cortés, leader of this Spanish expedition, under the direction of Diego Velasquez, governor of Cuba, proclaim possession of this land for King Charles the Fifth, the Holy Emperor of Spain." A cheer rose among the men as Cortés, the son of a poor country gentleman, took claim to a city said to be filled with gold.

Father Olmedo blessed the land for the good of their country then Malinche stepped forward to speak. She had grasped the sounds of the Spanish language from Cortés quickly, a true translator indeed, and Felipe was able to understand her message. "The city is spread in circles of jade, radiating flashes of light. Beside it the lords are carried in boats; over them extends a flowing mist."

Felipe looked toward the city. Green gardens lined the way toward the sparkling centerpiece edifice in the distance. The building towered above the land. What appeared to be a canal crossed the road a few feet in front of where he stood. A stream of men moved toward them. One of the men was carried on a litter. He wore embroidered robes and sandals adorned with gold. Feathers trailed from both the robes and his headdress.

Is this Moctezuma? Felipe wondered why the leader would greet them after the massacres that Cortés had ordered as they swept toward the inland. Would Moctezuma not fear for his own safety?

Malinche stood at the Spaniard's side as the litter drew near then dropped to her knees as though in prayer when the native was lowered for the men to speak. "It is the King."

"Moctezuma," Cortés said, bowing his head once briefly in acknowledgment.

"Quetzalcoatl," Moctezuma said.

Cortés did not correct the Mejicas leader.

Seeming to recognize the young woman still bowed at the white man's side, Moctezuma asked, "Malinche?" Felipe wondered how this king knew her name.

She raised her face toward the man. "Great Supreme Ruler."

At her words, Felipe noticed some of the creases across Moctezuma's forehead change from those which indicated worry, to a smile that washed across his face. He motioned for the woman to stand, which she did, staying at Cortés's side. A string of words Felipe did not understand came from Moctezuma, and the men accompanying him stepped toward Cortés, offering trays of sunflowers, jasmine, and magnolia flowers. The sweet odors wafted across the area where the men from both groups stood ready to attack if their leader's safety was threatened. The ruler placed garlands and golden bands around Cortés's neck and that of each of his officers. Wreaths were placed to adorn their heads.

The meeting appeared to be friendly. Felipe felt his spirit soar. Perhaps these two leaders would indeed come to an exchange that would be satisfying to them both. Malinche smiled as she spoke to Cortés, apparently explaining what each adornment meant.

Once the initial exchange finished, Cortés remounted his horse, and Moctezuma ordered his men to again lift the litter upon which he reclined. The two men led the procession toward the center of the city. Felipe fell into step behind the leader of his command, suspecting Cortés would be satisfied with nothing less than shiploads of gold to take back to Spain, and doubting that Moctezuma would be willing to supply them.

32

Tia's heart pounded in rhythm with the drums announcing Moctezuma's return. The white god and his men came with him into the palace courtyard. Quetzalcoatl's strange beast lumbered beside the guards who carried Moctezuma.

A low moan came from Rebekah, who stood next to her within the archway. At least Tia thought the noise came from her companion. The sound resonated so loud that it might have been coming from many of the women who had gathered, afraid to witness the arrival of the god, yet entranced enough to stay and bask in his presence.

Because she had already seen this man and those who followed him, she was past the initial fear the other women were surely now facing. She scanned the men, all dressed so differently from warriors who lived in Tenochtitlan. Breastplates shone beneath the garland draped around their necks. What she thought must be a protective head-cover covered some of their heads, but she noticed that only those men nearest the white god had helmet with the silver covering and a sharp point above their brows.

She strained to see those who walked behind the leader's beast. A sea of men filled the entire courtyard and beyond. Their skin color was lighter than her own, though not as light as their leader's. Were these yet another kind of god she had not learned about?

Their journey had been difficult, their tunics covered with stains, some dark enough to be dried blood. They stood in ranks as if readied for battle, but their necks bent and backs slumped, and with their weary eyes, the men looked as though they had no desire but to lie upon the ground and sleep for more than one passage of the moon.

She saw that most were older than she, except perhaps for the youth who tried to edge his way closer to the white god. If there were others near her own years, they were lost amid the throng. Suddenly, her eyes were drawn to the dark-haired woman hidden behind Quetzalcoatl. Bright patterns adorned the fabric of a skirt. The top of her garment was the faded color of grain left too long in the dry fields. When at last the woman turned, Tia recognized her friend, Malinche. How could this be? Older, yes, but still Malinche. There, at the god's side.

Tia stepped past Rebekah. "Our friend, Malinche, has come," Tia said, as she started to work her way through the doorway and into the crowd.

Rebekah was silent for a moment, the previous wail caught in her throat for a moment, then her words frantic, as though she wished to protect Tia from something. "No. Moctezuma is a fool to bring the white god into the palace grounds." She latched onto Tia's tunic, trying to hold her back. "It is a trick."

The king's litter had been lowered, and he stood on the far side of the courtyard at the palace entrance, prepared to welcome his honored guest.

"Allow the white god room to enter our palace courtyard!" His bellowed orders shook the servants from their frozen states, and the women scattered, nudging past Tia and Rebekah as they stood at the door to their quarters. The men ran into the palace through the other door.

"We must go." Rebekah gave another jerk on Tia's garment and held on.

Tia pulled loose. "What will it hurt if I stay?" Unsure where her sudden bravery had come from, she was certain she needed to hear the white god speak before she could allow herself to leave. She patted the younger girl's arm in a gesture of reassurance. "You go ahead. I will come soon."

Rebekah looked back and forth between Tia and the gate, then glanced toward the recesses of the palace itself, apparently unsure what to do. "But I . . ."

"Go on," Tia said, moving her hand in an urging motion. She wanted to see the reception Moctezuma gave the white god, and Rebekah's departure kept her from it.

Still appearing reluctant, Rebekah followed the last of the women through the archway. Tia turned again toward the main palace entrance. Additional gifts presented to Quetzalcoatl and the men who stood near him decorated their tunics. The others moved a few yards away toward the palaces of Axayacatl, Moctezuma's father. The white god and his men must be staying and needed places to rest.

To her surprise, Moctezuma followed along behind the

men. *He would never stay at his father's palaces–he considers them inferior to his own.* Cortés marched closely behind him, his hand held against Moctezuma's wrist. *Not of his own free will.* The two men looked like an oddly-placed couple engaged in a ritual dance.

With horror, she understood. A cold knowledge overtook her entire body. The great white god had taken Moctezuma prisoner. Because of Moctezuma's invitation to the palace, the stranger had taken them all prisoners. Although she had long been unhappy, sometimes even fearful for her life as his servant, at least she understood the ways of the Mejicas people. *What will the white god have in store for us?*

She slipped through the same doorway Rebekah had used to enter the palace but stayed close enough to watch the procession as Moctezuma's guards were escorted out, leaving the white god's men in their places. When the last man passed through the door, she retreated to tell the other women what she had witnessed. Rebekah had been right. It was a trick. But how was Malinche involved?

33

Never had Manuela imagined embroidery would be worth so much money. The earnings from the first sale had allowed her to purchase materials to double a new supply. Who cared that the women on the island had not been buying her work recently? She decided to concentrate on handkerchiefs again which took less time to make than the scarves and other things she had been making. The supply captain had been pleased with her wares, assuring that he would have no difficulty selling them.

Several more ships were preparing for departure to the European continent, and Manuela hoped she could persuade their pursers to buy even more. If she did, she would need to find a way to work more quickly, more efficiently. But the quality of her work must still be impeccable.

Always before, Manuela had sought inspiration to create a fresh design for each piece. Now she studied the bolt of finely woven cloth. She unbound several rounds, smoothing it against the surface of the dining table. A single square had been cut out already, leaving a strip wide and broad enough for four more squares. Old habits led her to cut a single square for the next handkerchief then an idea struck. *Why cut only one each time?* The wheels of her mind began to move as she realized precious stitching moments were used each time she retrieved the bolt, opened the fabric, cut a single piece then returned the bolt to the closet. *If I were to cut the entire bolt at once, think how much time I would save.* In a matter of minutes, several stacks of perfectly-cut squares sat atop the table.

If I could stitch them as quickly . . . And why not . . . Ideas began to churn. Although each step along the way must still be completed, additional time was wasted as she moved from one task to the next. Once hemming all of the new squares was completed, she would decide upon a design, gather threads and replace any missing colors before she sat to work. She glanced at her supplies. *Azul, verde, amarillo, negro*—all were low. A palate of other colors awaited her needle. A single needle. If it were misplaced, her work would be halted altogether until it was found or a new one obtained.

She began a mental list of things to purchase—five needles, color dyes, thread, perhaps an extra bolt of cloth. If her idea worked, she might complete many pieces each week instead of only a few.

"Manuela." Papa had arrived, the morning passed, and she had not noticed.

"Yes, Papa," she said as she hurried to the oven and pulled the freshly-baked bread from the rack above hot coals. Thankfully it was not burned. She sliced off a chunk, knowing he only allowed her to continue with the embroidery as long as it didn't interfere with his regular mealtimes. She slathered goat's butter across the steaming bread and added it to a saucer of sliced cheeses. Taking the saucer to the table, she set it before him then returned to cut herself a slice.

"My daughter," her father said when she came to the table with her own meal, "have you not made enough of these beautiful trinkets for the home you will share with César?"

The mention of his name never failed to stab both her heart and stomach. She paused before speaking, hoping the racing of her heart would calm. Her father didn't seem to notice and continued to eat, then swigged a drink of coffee to help wash it down.

At last she spoke. "I have long since completed the work for my own home." *With Felipe,* she added, but dared not mention his name until her plan was completed, with the dowry repayment saved and ready to present to her father in repayment for what he had given to César. The worry that her papa would refuse money from her continued, but she couldn't allow herself to dwell upon it.

He stood, his meal done. "Then why do you continue to sew, my little one?" He patted her on the top of the head like he had when she stood only at his knee, then he left the house to return to his work.

Although she felt relief that he didn't wait for an answer, color still rushed into her cheeks as she stood, her mouth agape. *Little one? Has he not eyes to see?* She wore the full figure of a woman. Her heart was no longer the playful one of a child, and she had given it to Felipe, not to César. She carried herself in dignity, like her mother had as the head of a household. *I am grown.* Her resolve faltered only a moment as she realized this had made no difference in the life of her mother. She, Manuela, would not be ruled by the whims of men. *I will make my own choices, just as I will make my own money to support them.*

34

Two hundred sixty-six men readied horses, weapons, and supply packs to return to Veracruz since word had come from a supply ship that the governor of Cuba sent soldiers to arrest Cortés for insubordination. Felipe assisted with the preparations. Staying behind at the palace with Captain de Alvarado seemed a better assignment than going with de Narvaez back to Veracruz. Felipe anticipated a chance to explore the opulent palace gardens and finery within the gates. Perhaps he would also venture into the city. The tall pyramid structures he had marched past piqued his interest.

Narvaez's group departed, the dust settled, leaving Felipe standing in center of the palace courtyard, basking in the warm sun and breathing in the moist morning air. He closed his eyes and the images within his mind were of home—Cuba. Manuela. Her olive skin against the pale linen blouse she wore loose around her shoulders. Her long skirt, woven of brightly-colored threads—orange, yellow, red—barely covering the delicate toes which wiggled against her leather sandals. The sun again beat upon him in the city square of Cuba where he stood on the hill he had claimed in so many childhood battles. A familiar giggle almost convinced him he had somehow dreamed all that had happened the past months.

At last he opened his eyes, but the dark-haired beauty who stood before him was not Manuela. Pieces of her clothing were similar—bare toes against woven sandal, heavy pale fabric in a cloth tunic that reached to her ankles. She appeared to be about the same age Manuela would now be, a budding beauty, ready for marriage.

Perhaps the girl realized Felipe stared at her because a long rush of words from her—nothing he recognized though—were directed at him. Felipe shook his head in an effort to concentrate on what she said. Was she berating him for all that Cortés had done to her people? Would she attack him? She didn't seem angry, but Felipe was sure the ways of her people were nothing like those of his own.

"I . . ." Felipe didn't know words to continue. No cohesive question could form in his mind. It didn't matter. He couldn't understand her, and he was certain she wouldn't be able to understand him. The girl began again, the words offered more slowly this time, but Felipe still did not know what she said.

"*Cihuätl . . . calli . . .*" She pointed toward the second palace where Felipe and the other Spaniards had slept since they had arrived. "*Malinche?*"

Malinche? Felipe recognized the sound of this word. Did it mean something, or was this slave girl referring to the young woman Cortés had taken as not only his interpreter, but now as his wife?

"Yes, Malinche," Felipe said, nodding his head, hoping to let the girl know he recognized the word and could take her to the woman Cortés referred to by that name.

A smile burst across the slave's face as Felipe turned to lead her across the courtyard. *Indeed*, he thought, *she is so like Manuela*. In a familiar gesture, he touched the girl's hand, but she immediately pulled back. The smile disappeared and fear crossed her face.

"*Idiota!*" Felipe almost spat the word intended toward himself.

"I couldn't agree more." César stood in the archway which led to the second palace. He leaned against the stone pillar, relaxed, his arms crossed at his waist. His jaw was thrust forward, and he moved his head as he eyed the local beauty who now cowered behind Felipe. "I see you have found a fine replacement for the woman I intend to make my wife."

A sudden insight and memory flashed through Felipe's mind. Perhaps it wasn't *his* gesture that had frightened the girl, but César's, just as it had been at their last encounter with Manuela. Like she had done then, this Mejicas slave moved closer to Felipe, gently touching the shoulder of his tunic as if to gain strength from the garment.

"Leave her alone, César," Felipe said, his tone firm and commanding.

"That depends on which one you want me to leave alone." César chuckled. "Unless of course, I decide to make both of them my own."

In one step, Felipe was away from the girl. His right arm

swung toward César's face, and the punch delivered. The speed of his response surprised even Felipe. César was covered in blood which flowed from his nose. His feet splayed in front of him as he sat where he had fallen. Felipe grabbed the girl's hand, and they moved past the archway before César could recover.

Although Felipe knew she didn't understand him, the heat of the moment caused him to continue to babble. "Arrogant *pinga*. To think I used to fear his swaggering bravado. He is nothing, no threat to me. I was a child to let him badger me so." She stumbled, but righted herself quickly because Felipe continued to pull her along.

They entered the palace door, Felipe passing the Spanish guard with no challenge, although he did notice the smile play upon the man's lips as the girl followed close behind. "And you." He threw the words back over his shoulder toward the guard. "Another *pinche bastardo*," Felipe said as they continued through the open entryway and toward the sleeping quarters at the back. "Think what you want, but none of it will be true."

He slammed his fist against several of the doors as he strode past, the slave girl struggling to keep up with his pace. One or two doors opened, and Cortés's men peered into the hallway, following their progress as Felipe called out, "Malinche? Has anyone seen the woman named *Malinche*?"

The door at the end of the passage opened, and there she stood, a golden shawl draped across her shoulders. Her hair was swept up and adorned with a comb at the crown of her head. *No wonder Cortés had taken her as his bride*, Felipe thought. *She is beautiful.*

163

He let go of the slave girl's hand as she ran the remaining steps until the two women embraced, holding each other for a long time. *They were both beautiful,* Felipe thought. *But no more so than Manuela.* He felt drawn to these two women, and somehow safe, not wanting to leave their presence.

Tia hugged Malinche like a long-gone sister, allowing words to pour from her mouth like water from an overflowing jug. "I recognized you when you arrived. Why are you with the great White God? Is it the same god you told me my parents believed in? Why does he overtake the palace of Moctezuma, despite the gifts and offerings he has been given? Are we all really his prisoners?"

"Hush. Hush," Malinche said, pulling away from her as though to get a better look. "You seem well. Always a good sign in the house of Moctezuma."

The warm chuckle that came from her lips reminded Tia of the pleasant says they had spent together before the woman's departure.

Malinche looked past Tia toward the youth who had brought Tia to her.

He spoke in the language of Cortés. "You are the woman known as *Malinche,* are you not?"

"I am. Won't you join us?" Malinche extended her hand to welcome the young man into her chambers.

"But Cortés . . ." he said, starting to deny her request.

"Please, don't worry," Malinche said. "He has a battle to

be won, and the spoils to divide. He will be gone several days. No harm will befall you here."

Tia immediately thought of the other young man, the one sitting in the courtyard, blood pouring from his nose. Would he try to follow them to Malinche's chambers? She again took hold of Felipe's hand, this time to pull him through the doors so that Malinche could shut out the world behind them.

"You have returned just in time to celebrate the Feast of Huitzilopochtli," Tia said to Malinche as she led Felipe across the room and took a seat on a cushioned divan. The young man looked around as though he didn't know what to do.

"*Tomar asiento*," Malinche said to him. He immediately looked grateful and took a place on a nearby couch. "*Ätl?*" she said to Tia as she poured water into an ornate cup from a decanter on the table. Tia nodded then reached for the cup. Malinche turned to the Spaniard. "Agua?"

"Gracias," he said as he took a cup.

She tried saying the word Malinche had used. *Agua*. The sound felt strange against her lips, yet the process was familiar as she remembered the many words practiced with Malinche's careful tutoring in the weeks she had been here before.

The young man must have figured out what Tia was doing when she said his word *agua* because he pointed to his own cup and said *ätl*. The word was recognizable, if not exactly the way she would lift her tongue away from the final sound. It was a start. The two of them had one word in common, and she could hardly wait to sort out the untold numbers more they would learn with Malinche there to help them.

35

Manuela couldn't believe how quickly the handkerchiefs were completed now. She had whipped the edges of the squares into a hem before placing delicate flowers of many colors into one corner. At the end of a single week over thirty of the simple patterns were finished. She had made an additional five pieces with a flock of birds soaring over the ocean, and one pattern had the lines of the ship that had taken away Felipe.

As she lay another completed piece aside, Manuela heard Eduardo's familiar voice outside her window. He was talking with someone. *Papa?*

"Still no word from Captain Cortés and his expedition, Señor," Eduardo said.

Manuela was surprised by the deep tones of his voice, which no longer cracked when he spoke. He had been such a child when the ships left the harbor. Now, two years later, a fair-haired beard adorned his face. The muscles of his arms and chest were more defined, and he stood taller than she.

"When were you last at the docks?" Papa asked. His voice too came from just outside the window.

"This morning," Eduardo said. "I go every morning. I want to be there when the triumphant men return."

So wrapped up in her own worries over the years, Manuela had not recognized her best friend and confidant was also maturing. Eduardo had become much more than a friend through the trial she faced. She had found him to be quick and shrewd when it came to business dealings, especially while bartering with the ship pursers. She had asked him to help again so she could spend more time sewing.

She stood to greet them as they entered the door. "Papa," she said, giving her customary curtsy. "Eduardo." She smiled, perhaps something she had not done enough over the long months.

Eduardo pulled his head back, a look of surprise crossing his face, probably because of her smile, Manuela thought.

"Manuela, you look well this beautiful day," Eduardo said. His eyes lingered over her face.

A blush of warmth rose in her cheeks. A little flutter clutched her heart. And her skin tingled as though she had been touched. *Not since Felipe left have I felt . . . No . . . I have only missed . . .* Deep in her soul, Manuela loved Felipe, but how could she not help the feelings caused by the smile of a handsome young man? She had no reason to avoid flirting. Especially if that young man were as good a friend as Eduardo.

It felt good to flirt a little, Manuela decided. But the yearning she still felt for Felipe told her it would not be wise to play with the affections of his best friend. Eduardo was a true friend. His concern regarding Felipe was as real as her own, and Eduardo's business sense had allowed Manuela to amass more than enough money to buy back her dowry.

Her apology had not been swift, "I'm sorry, Eduardo."

"For what?" He was the model of perfect innocence. He rubbed the palm of his hand across his chin.

Even if he understood she had been flirting—and she was not sure that he did—she realized he would never mention it for fear of embarrassing her further. Time would pass and things would remain the same between them, although today she needed to talk again with Eduardo about the money she had been making at selling her wares to the merchant ships. And later, later she would again speak with her papa.

With her money counted and tallies memorized, and since Eduardo had gone, the time was right for Manuela to speak with her father, letting him know what she intended to do. Papa was fair in his dealings with the other local farmers; he dealt often with merchants and was well-respected by them. Surely he would hear the pleas of his own beloved child when it came to the matter of her marriage bans.

Then again, he had not listened before when she tried to convince him that she could not marry César. She could not stand another word of praise for him. "Enough!" she had muttered, although she wanted to shout the word, then leave to sit for hours at the water's edge, hoping for some glimmer of sun against the white sails of an incoming ship. When she did see one, Manuela had trouble holding her heart in check, praying the boat would be part of Cortés' entourage, but knowing she would likely be disappointed.

She planned to meet her father in the hillside terraces where he spent most of his time. She had often visited him among the sheep when she was a young and knew he was more relaxed when among the herd, more willing to listen to childish chatter and entertain her ideas. *Perhaps this time he will listen about canceling this marriage and allowing me to marry Felipe.*

The last time she mentioned it, her father had scoffed, saying, "Felipe will never provide anything to care for a wife. He has no money, no land, and no hope of obtaining a herd."

Now that she had money, Manuela didn't think any of her papa's arguments mattered. Her skills would allow them to have enough until Felipe could establish himself as a herder. Perhaps he would come home with wealth of his own. He might at least be paid for his work. But if not, nothing mattered except that he returned.

Manuela passed the low walls that separated Papa's land from that of the neighbors, the gentle slope of the meadowland dotted with rocky patches. The dark rich soil between the stones provided the perfect breeding ground for the ginger lily that had sprung up in recent days. She noticed the white flowers against the dark slope from the hillside near their house.

The sheep grazed and Papa napped when Manuela arrived. He lay on the hillside on his back, great snorts coming from his mouth as he slept. She held in a laugh, not wanting to wake him. She sat beside him and studied his face. *When did your beard turn white? And the wrinkles around your eyes are deeper. Your tanned skin looks like leather. Papa, when did you turn so old?* A sudden fear hit her. *Will you live to see my children?*

"How long before the time comes that you will leave me?" she whispered. Her mama was young when she passed from this life. Only a few more than twenty years, Papa said. Manuela had been a small child less than ten when her mother's fever came. It took only days . . .

A quick glance at her papa made Manuela shake off her worry. Of course he would not die. Not for many, many years. Her husband would support her and care for her aging parent so that Papa did not need to continue to work among the sheep. Or if Felipe did not, she would. *Does any other woman in all of Cuba have as much money as I have saved?* Manuela doubted it.

The tingling of a ram's bell startled her—and her father, too. He sat up and looked around as though he didn't know where he was. He rubbed the sleep from his eyes then he saw her and opened his arms wide. "Manuela, what are you doing here?"

"Can I not come visit my *papito* who works so hard?" Manuela reached over to give him a little peck upon the cheek. "You never complained when I came as a child." She added a quick hug then settled into a comfortable spot.

171

"Nor do I complain now," he said, rubbing his eyes again as though to help them focus. He produced a great yawn, which ended in a wide smile. Manuela dug into her pocket and pulled a crusted roll. She offered it to him. "Thank you, my dear one." He took a bite and chewed thoroughly before swallowing, then took a second bite.

"Papa . . ." Manuela had thought through what she wanted to say, but she was hesitant to begin. *What if he won't listen to me, just like those other times?* But she hoped while he was relaxed from his nap might be the time to convince him. He looked at her, his eyebrows raised in a question, obviously waiting to hear what she had to say. "Papa, I know you have seen my embroidery work."

He took another bite, chewed then spoke over a mouthful. "It's beautiful, like the work of your mother. It's for your dowry, and the home you will build with César."

"No, Papa. No." Manuela took a deep breath then rushed through the words she had practiced over and over in her mind. "My dowry is not for a home with César. Anything I prepare is for the home I will someday have with Felipe." She could see the word *no* form on her father's lips, but she continued. "And most of the pieces I have been making are not mine at all. I have sold them. They have gone on ships toward Europe and the motherland, and the money . . . the money I have been saving is now enough to replace what you gave to César's mother as my dowry."

The jovial look on his face changed to one of anger. "You have money, of your own? And the dowry . . . We have discussed this before." He started to rise as though to walk away.

172

Manuela put out her hand to stop him. "No, Papa. We have *not* discussed this. You have given a decree, and I have been ignored." She removed her hand from his arm and stood. "I am now a wealthy woman. I have more than enough to repay you, and with money left over."

He scrambled to his feet and jutted his chin out toward her as he spoke. "A wealthy woman? Ha! Do you even know what wealth means, my dear child?" The fire in his eyes proved his displeasure.

"As I have said, I have the entire repayment for the dowry monies you gave to César's mother. I have several nuggets of silver and gold, plus enough coin to cover the needs for both me and Felipe for a year." She could see her father's face change emotion, the look of frustration melting to wonder. Her voice remained soft as she continued. "And I own land. Several acres, Papa. I have the deeds."

He stepped back, as though stunned by the information. He placed his hand against his chest above his heart. "I don't understand. You are serious about breaking the bonds, because you have no need?" He shook his head and the confusion showed in his dark eyes.

"No, Papa. Because I have no love. César has always frightened me." She lowered her head, brushing her hand across her brow before letting it settle against her mouth. She took a deep breath before lifting her eyes. "Marrying him would make me unhappy."

"I had no idea you felt that way. Have I been so blind?" Her papa touched her arm. "What has he done to you? Why are you afraid?" He stepped forward and placed his arm around her shoulder.

"He has not harmed me, Papa, but César is a bully, and I fear he will mistreat me as he so often mistreats others. I am only safe when I am with Felipe. It is Felipe I love, and him I wish to marry."

Her father took her into a full hug, patting her back like he had when she was little. "I am so sorry, Manuela, that I did not listen before. We will take care of this as soon as these young men return home from their journey, I promise."

Her relief was overwhelming as she felt it rush through her entire body. Tears of joy sprang to her eyes. "Thank you, Papa. Thank you."

A deep chuckle rose from his throat as he held her close for one more squeeze. "My daughter is a wealthy woman. Who ever would have guessed?" He released her to look into her eyes. "But not as wealthy as her papa, who has such a daughter to call his own."

37

In the weeks his leader had been gone, Felipe enjoyed spending time with both Malinche and Tia, who reminded him so much of Manuela in the way she laughed, tossed her hair, and the smile that burst upon her face when she was pleased with herself. With the Mejicas leader still in confinement, little work seemed to be moving forward in the grand palace. Both slave girls were free to spend time showing Felipe around the grounds and the city of Tenochtitlan.

In addition to exploring the tunnels within the main palace and their underground connections to the other four buildings on the square, Felipe began to learn why the Mejicas people had reacted with submission and honor toward the Spaniards' arrival in their capital city. Malinche had helped him learn a few words of the native language, but Tia had been much quicker catching on to Spanish and the three of them were soon able to communicate.

They stood before the temple of Huitzilopochitli. A ribbon of color flowed from the top of the temple steps to the narrow trough below. Felipe recognized the deep red stains at once as he neared the temple steps. *Blood!* How many men must have died to tint the saturated stone to the color of copper?

"Your *nantli* believes Cortés is Quetzalcoatl?" Felipe asked Tia.

"No, my *nantli*—mother—believes that the great white god Quetzalcoatl will return to this land as he declared," she explained, her voice patient as if she were explaining to a very small child. "Moctezuma believes that your leader, Cortés, is this god who has come to claim his rightful place, removing Moctezuma as the leader of this country, a feat he has already performed."

Malinche shook her head. After only a few months as Cortés's wife, the young woman constantly wore a tired look upon her face. The battles had already been too much for her to bear. "Unfortunately, Cortés is all too willing to let this deception continue. His lust for gold is stronger than even his concern for me."

The two young women moved several steps away from the temple, and Felipe followed. Tia placed her hand at the nape of Malinche's neck, smoothing the hairs which had fallen loose from the bun, then spoke. "The desire for gold has driven many men to their deaths." Her gaze flickered toward Felipe for a moment. "Do you know what Cortés has planned for our city and its leader upon his return?"

"He told us nothing of his plans," Felipe said before Malinche could answer. "But I confirm his lust for gold. He has promised us each a portion, and he plans to buy the approval of Spain's king and queen. Of course, Cortés also hopes to bear home to the motherland a wealth of gold for himself." He stepped into a bow, showing his respect for Malinche. "And I am also sure, a queenly sum for his bride."

Malinche let a hint of a smile grace her lips, but again shook her head in denial. She took a seat on the broad rim of a fountain. "A beautiful gesture, Felipe, but nothing shines as brightly in Cortés's heart as gold."

Tia sat beside her and patted the stone, indicating that Felipe should also rest.

They sat in silence for awhile. Felipe enjoyed the beating sun, warm against his skin. He took a deep breath, wondering why the hint of ash seemed strong across the sky again. The dark smoke which had covered the blue on the day of his arrival in Tenochtitlan had ended once Cortés had taken Moctezuma prisoner. Felipe had asked several days ago about the stench coming from the fires.

"Human flesh," Malinche had told him.

"Sacrifices to the god Huitzilopochitli," Tia had added. "Moctezuma sends hundreds of men and women from the top of the temple to their death, hoping the sacrificial offering to this god will prevent Quetzalcoatl from conquering the land."

What? Felipe couldn't image the horror of human sacrifices, no matter who the god they were intended to please. The temple was only paces from where Felipe now sat. He squinted briefly into the afternoon sun then turned his face easterly, a twinge of homesickness piercing his breast. A thread of white smoke wended across the azure sky. He allowed his eyes to trace its source—the top of the temple.

"Look up there," he said, pointing toward the flames that were just becoming visible.

Tia gasped and touched her hand at the base of her throat as she stared at the smoke above her. "How can this be? Why are sacrifices starting again?"

"Do you suppose Moctezuma has somehow escaped his bondage?" Malinche asked.

"No," Felipe said, his voice firm, but his concern heightened. Across the courtyard, he saw a group of men from his own crew. Each prodded before him a native with their darker skin and loincloths. Captain Alvarado sat astride a roan-colored steed. The captain held his sword at the ready. "This time it may be the Spanish who have turned toward the temple as their source of strength."

"We must return to the palace," Malinche said, shaking Felipe from his concentration.

"Yes. Neither of you is safe." Although he could only guess what Alvarado had as his intentions, Felipe recognized that the young women's copper color put them in jeopardy if they were spotted by the group of men now mounting the temple steps.

"This way," Tia said as she led the way around the fountain and down a path Felipe had never taken before. She hurried toward the archway marking the end of the narrow passageway, he and Malinche both following her closely.

"Where are you off to in such a hurry?" César stepped from a side passage directly into Tia's path, halting their retreat.

A gasp escaped from both women's lips. Felipe moved in front of them, pulling to his full height in Césars face. "Out of our way, or I'll deliver another punch like the one I gave you the last time we met."

César flinched, even if ever so slightly. "Under the command of General Alvarado . . . I . . . I order you to deliver these two *slaves* to the temple . . . for a sacrifice."

"Sacrifice? Now that Cortés is gone, does Alvarado believe himself to be the great white god, to order such a ceremony as this? Would he dare order the sacrifice of Cortés's new wife?" Felipe asked. Surely Alvarado wouldn't dare touch her.

He became aware of the sound of angry voices in the corridor toward the city square. Not sure how much time he would have before the other men discovered them, and he would lose Tia and Malinche forever, Felipe tried to push past César, but was stopped by his next comment.

"He would sacrifice her for gold," César said. "Gold is the only thing that matters. Alvarado has guaranteed us more gold than even Cortés could deliver."

Felipe glanced at the two women. The younger one held the arm of the elder. Both wore the same expression as earlier when they talked of this lust destroying many men.

"And what will you do with your share of this gold, César?" Felipe said, almost anticipating what the answer would be.

"I will return and give it to Manuela."

Despite his dire circumstances, Felipe stifled a chuckle before he said, "You cannot buy her love."

"No woman's love can be bought with a handful of gold," Tia said, her Spanish surprisingly accurate. "Passion of the heart can only be secured with an equal measure of love."

"Come," Malinche said as she took both Tia and Felipe's hands and led them past the stunned César, toward Moctezuma's palace.

38

"Over six hundred people were sacrificed." Felipe kept his voice low as he spoke with Tia inside the palace courtyard. "Alvarado seized all of the gold Moctezuma gave Cortés. Do not leave the garden gates, or they might take you as well."

She searched for the words to ask, "Al-va-ra-do? He is the man at the temple?" Although she had learned many more words in her conversations with Felipe, she still struggled to remember every word, most of them unnatural to her tongue.

"Yes, the man who made the sacrifices," Felipe said. He glanced behind him—the temple was visible in the distance—then returned his full attention to what she was saying.

"No, no," she continued. "The man who talked to us." She held a hand up as if to indicate height, then shaped a body broader than the captain's. "The same old . . . age . . . as you."

Felipe's eyebrows furrowed as he frowned. "César."

"That one," she said. Her eyes lit in recognition of the name, but her lips trembled. "He tried to come in the palace. Queen Aramonia ordered him away from her." Her arm made a swift movement, finger outstretched toward the gate. The message her eyes flashed was stern, as though she would not take *no* for an answer.

Felipe reached out to touch her arm, drawing in a deep breath. "And he left?" If her imitation was accurate, the queen was a strong woman, not afraid of confrontation with the enemy, even though she was a prisoner.

Tia nodded her head vigorously. "I didn't understand the words he said, but he left the gates and joined others who waited." She pointed to a spot a few paces down the wall. "I went into the garden and listened through the ivy. They talked of gold."

"The gold from Moctezuma himself, no doubt." Felipe dropped his hand from her arm, a tingle passing through him as he thought how smooth her skin was under his touch. Suddenly he felt warm. He fanned a gnat away from his brow, hoping to cool the emotion that had enveloped him.

"They also spoke of sil . . . ver." Tia hesitated a second then spoke the word again. "Silver. What is silver?" She cocked her head to the side and rolled her eyes like she was searching her memory to find the meaning, a gesture that seemed to make the slave girl even more beautiful than he had noticed before.

"Shiny metal," he said, "like gold, but more like the sparkle of water against the bay." For a moment, he could not bring a picture of Manuela to his mind. He wondered how she looked after all this time. He knew he had changed, matured. Surely, she too had grown and become more beautiful.

"Is *silver* wanted by your leader?"

He was startled from his thoughts. "Very much. He wants both gold and silver to take to his king and queen . . . but mostly for himself, I think," Felipe said. "He has told us that he will share his wealth once he collects riches from the people of this land. I don't believe him."

"He won't have to work so hard to gather this silver and gold, I think," Tia said. Felipe raised his eyebrows, and his mouth formed a little O as she continued. "Alvarado's men have done it for him." She leaned forward, as though she were sharing a secret.

"Why do you say this?" Felipe asked.

"César. He said *silver* and *gold* while coming to palace. I do not know what he means, so I waited until all the men were gone then I asked Aramonia." She stood up straight again, head held high as though she were proud of what she had done.

"*The queen?*" Felipe swallowed too deep and began to cough. He bent at his waist and pounded his hands against his breast, but the wracking overtook his body for several moments.

Tia pulled him toward the fountain in the center of the courtyard and cupped her hands, filling them with water, which she lifted to his mouth over and again.

As he sipped the cool liquid from her palms, the coughing quieted, and he was at last able to regain his words. "You asked the queen?"

"Why wouldn't I ask?" she said, as if his question were absurd. She dried her hands against the flaxen tunic she wore.

"If you speak to her—especially to ask a question—does she not punish you?"

"I know Aramonia since I was a babe. She cared for me before she was Moctezuma's wife." Tia made a clicking sound with her mouth and swung her head back and forth to show her displeasure for a moment before she again spoke. "She used to treat me as little sister. Now my duties are light, but still service of queen."

Concern drew Felipe's face into a frown again. "Nothing like the rule of her husband, then."

"Nothing like her husband," she said.

Noise outside the gate drew Felipe's attention. He walked across the courtyard to a place where he could see the street.

Tia followed. "He sends messengers to other tribal leaders, told to gather all gold and silver. Bring to palace as tribute."

"But this action is under the order of Cortés," Felipe said. "Not Moctezuma. My captain told us that Cortés has set aside some of the spoil to go to Ferdinand and Isabella. The remaining is what he promises to share with his men."

A scream pierced the air. Felipe reacted by urging Tia further into the courtyard. "Stay back. I must see what is happening." He returned to the gate and poked his head out to see a swarm of Spanish men, wearing breastplates of armor and carrying Mejicas spears, run toward the city square. Dust rose under their feet, blocking the temple which Felipe had been able to see before.

"*Kill him. Kill him.*" The rumbling message gained strength as the horde continued to pour toward the temple. "*He has returned. Vengeance is ours.*"

Others from the palace rushed to see what the noise might mean. Both men and women slaves hurried across the courtyard, making their way toward the gated opening, trying to see into the street beyond. Tia was pushed from the safety of the courtyard and into the street directly behind Felipe. She grabbed onto his tunic so that she wasn't forced to the ground and trampled beneath the running feet.

"Kill him," the soldiers continued to yell as they moved toward the city square. "This way."

"What is it? What do they say?" Tia yelled above the din. "Why do they run to temple?"

"I'm not sure," Felipe said. "Stop" he yelled, hoping to catch the attention of one of the passing soldiers. He recognized a burly man from the mast ship. "Jésu!"

Jésu was near the end of the pack of men and must have heard or seen Felipe. He slowed for a moment.

"Kill who?" Felipe called.

The soldier looked toward Felipe, Tia, and the group huddled around the gate. "Cortés," he said then sped up to join the departing group.

The stench of burning flesh made Felipe's nostrils sting as if the fire had climbed within them. He stood at the base of the temple where blood continued to drain from above. Tears welled in his eyes, making it difficult for him to see. A mass of humanity swarmed around him, and the shouting voices called men first to battle on one side, then to the opposition. Blood covered the ground at his feet and across the plaza. He tried to remain focused, but the thought of killing anyone, much less fighting against the men he had worked alongside, made his stomach roil like it did when he first awoke onboard the ship.

How has it come to this? Cuban against Cuban, Spaniard against Spaniard, with Mejicas against them all. He remained true to Cortés, believing the captain would be the only one capable of taking them back home to Cuba. But so many of his shipmates had joined forces with Alvarado, as César had done.

Their lust for gold pushing them into mutiny.

A man with a broadsword rushed toward him. Felipe recognized him as one of Alvarado's group. He raised his own sword. Metal clashed against metal as they met.

Ugh! A rush of air came from Felipe. He lunged and brought the sword edge into a second crash against the weapon of the sailor who had become his enemy. The man spun from the force of the blow, and Felipe knew he must maintain his advantage or die. He reached out with his foot, swiping it against the Spaniard's foot. The man lost his balance, backing into César.

"Damn!" Felipe cried. Now he must fight not only this man, but also César. Except both César and the other Spaniard fell to the dirt. Felipe used the interruption to his advantage.

He ran.

Thoughts flooded his mind as he dodged through the warriors—hundreds of them it seemed—and fled away from the temple plaza toward the palace. *I must escape. Why did I ever want to leave Cuba?*

Across the square, a pile of bodies blocked his path through the narrow street passage. Choking back the sour taste that rose in his mouth, he started to climb them as though he were scaling the temple walls. Other men's blood, left from the wounds the warriors had suffered before they died, coated his palms. The odor of decay mixed with the burning smell. Tears washed his eyes, and his tongue fought to remove the flavor of the rancid flavor from his mouth. Still he forced himself to scale the dead, seeking the only way out from the public square.

As he reached the top, ready to throw himself to the other side, Felipe felt a tug against the hem of his tunic. Images of dead men rising up to bring him into the depths of hell flashed through his mind. Sudden panic caught in his heart, but he forced his face to turn to see what had snagged the cloth and found himself face to face with a dark-skinned man—a Mejicas native who had climbed up behind him. His face was covered by slashes of white which caused his mouth to look like he bore the teeth of a tiger. He gripped the tunic in one hand and held a knife in the other.

"Let go!" Felipe yelled, hoping the tone of his voice would make the man understand even though he didn't know the words. "Release me!" He pulled his sword lose from his belt and raised it.

He didn't understand the guttural words that came from the native, but he knew the intention. The hand bearing the knife shot into the air and started an arc toward him. Before he could react, Felipe heard a gasp emerge from the man, as though he were suddenly fighting for air. The native's legs collapsed, and he fell forward. A double-handed sword protruded from his back.

César stood over him. Hope, then fear rushed through Felipe as he fought to stand, wielding his own weapon. "Have you come to finish me off, then, for yourself?"

"Fool!" César said, his tone softer—more gentle perhaps—than Felipe ever remembered hearing it. "Come. We must escape from this pit of death." He offered his outstretched hand. "This battle is insanity."

A moment's hesitation, a battle within his mind won by his own more-gentle self, Felipe took the offer, and the two of them made a hasty descent from the mound of bodies and ran through the streets toward Moctezuma's palace to what he hoped was safety. But if Alvarado's side won—or Moctezuma's—he doubted the palace would offer much solace to anyone who still supported Cortés and his mission.

"Why?" Felipe managed to ask. His breathing was ragged, the air and energy sucked from him after the ordeal in the plaza. "Why did you save me?" The garden gates were in view. In his mind, he could almost smell the wild orchids surrounding the stone entrance.

"No gold is worth the slaughter we just left," César said. "Without our lives, what good does any of it do for us? I'm sorry . . . so sorry I tried to come . . . between you and Manuela."

His voice sounded repentant. How had César changed so in the midst of battle? The sounds of rage had become faint behind them. Felipe glanced upward in a silent prayer of thanks then focused again on the gates. Tia stood thirty yards away in the archway, her hand raised to her cover her lips. Her eyes were wide in terror. A glance over his shoulder told Felipe they had escaped. He saw no one following behind them. Nearly out of breath, he slowed his pace.

César did the same as he continued, "I know now that love is more important than anything, especially more important than the search for gold."

He listened to César with hope in his heart that all would be well. Only another fifty steps and they would be within the walls. The steady rhythm of their feet lulled him into a sense of security, a feeling of bravery. He waved to Tia who was motioning them forward. He mouth was open like she called to them, but he couldn't hear her words.

"Manuela does not love me. She loves you." César stopped moving forward, and Felipe halted also. The battle seemed so far behind them. "When we return to Cuba, I will repay the dowry, and Manuela will be free to become your bride."

Never would he have expected those words from César, who only moments ago was his enemy. *Manuela will be mine with no struggle?* Felipe felt as though he had been struck dumb.

"Felipe!" Tia's shrill voice cut into his thoughts.

A warrior's scream came from behind them. Felipe heard the thud as a *macuahuitl* whacked César in the back of

189

the head. César dropped to the ground. A stream of blood pooled from the spot where his head lay. A weapon lay at Felipe's feet, Tia stood before him, and he saw a painted Mejicas warrior, a flow of unfamiliar angry-sounding words spouting from his mouth, running toward them from the direction of the city. A knife was held in his left hand.

"Come!" Tia said as she grabbed Felipe's hand.

How was she here? When did she come into the street? Then another unexpected thought. *We can't leave César.*

As she pulled Felipe into the garden, several of the male household servants gathered around them. "*Enemigo,*" she said in a word Felipe understood. *Enemy.*

She pointed toward the outer courtyard beyond the gate, and to the man running toward them. One of the servants pulled a weapon—like one he had seen in the hands of a Spaniard—and a shot rang out.

The man in the street fell to the earth—dead.

40

Tia held Felipe's hand as they hurried across the courtyard toward the servants' palace entrance. He was no longer safe at Moctezuma's residence. She must take him across the land bridge then send him toward the ships on the great water. She didn't know if he could cross the great waters alone, but he needed to try.

"Where are we going?" Felipe asked as they passed those whom he had come to know through her friendship—Jeroni the cook, Tia's friend Rebekha, even Malinche stood unmoving near the baking ovens as Tia pulled him through the kitchen area.

"This way," she said without answering the question in the manner she knew he wanted. A series of marble steps lead to a lower level of the palace. She hoped she could remember the path through the tunnel system away from Moctezuma's quarters. Felipe's only hope at survival was to get him away from both the Mejicas and the Spaniards who were slaughtering each other.

The palace opulence became more evident as they worked their way from the servants' wing into the supreme ruler's. Although she was familiar with the decorative gold within the shrines and idols, she knew that Felipe was not. His slowing pace made it evident that he was intrigued by the golden or wood pieces they passed. Intricate carvings of the great white god Quetzalcoatl lined the walls. Statuary depicted the arrival of the man Moctezuma revered as God—surely not Cortés since these pieces were much older.

"We must hurry," Tia said.

"These ships." Felipe let go of her hand and stopped in front of a carving. "They look like the ones we sailed in from Cuba."

She placed her hand against his upper arm. "They represent the ships that carried Quetzalcoatl, the Great White God. Moctezuma believes that your leader, Cortés, fulfills his promised return."

"Yes, you've told me this before." Confusion still marked Felipe's face as he wrinkled his brow and chewed on his lower lip briefly before continuing. "Ships from Spain carry the same markings as these have along the stern. Do you think . . . Of course the white god would have no need of ships if he were indeed a god . . . even the ruler at the time of Quetzalcoatl's first coming . . . perhaps *he* was fooled?"

A feeling of relief washed through her at his words, but she didn't understand it. She had known all along that Cortés was not the Great White God. But never had she considered that Quetzalcoatl himself was not a god either. Then who did her parents believe would come to save the world? Was there another god in whom she should believe?

192

"We must hurry," she said again. She reached for Felipe's hand. The hallway would eventually take them to the outside walls and a narrow tributary where the ruler kept a boat. She had seen Moctezuma and two of the priests sail away under the power of a single slave. She knew Felipe would be able to handle the boat by himself and that the river channel would lead him toward safety.

She continued to mull the question about God. Was there such a being? What did it matter to her, she who was nothing more than a slave?

"Tia!" In the middle of the tunnel, Queen Aramonia stood, hands on hips and rage on her face. "Where are you going? What are you doing in this part of the palace?" She hesitated before continuing with, "And who is this you are taking into the private recesses of the Supreme Ruler?"

"My queen," Tia said, stopping in front of her with a bow to one knee. "Our people fight against the forces of the white god as these strangers fight against each other. Felipe . . ." Tia rose and moved her hand to indicate the young man who stood behind her, ". . . is my friend. Listen to him, please."

Before Queen Aramonia could deny him the privilege, Felipe spoke in her language. "Tenochtitlan is lost. The city is in ruins. Blood pours from the temple steps, and fires blaze through the square. Men are slaughtered in the streets like cattle prepared for a feast. No one is safe, and soon the battle will rage in the courtyard even within the palace gates."

Aramonia pulled her hands to cover her silent scream.

"My husband . . ." She glanced toward his chambers, but looked right back at Tia. This time her eyes were widened, and the color was blanched from her face.

"Go find him," Tia said. In her heart she knew there was nothing he could do, but she must lead Felipe away from the palace, and Aramonia still blocked the path.

The queen nodded and turned toward a side corridor then began to run. Tia and Felipe did the same, covering the last few steps to the door. Once outside, she located the boat immediately. "There," she cried as she pointed to a structure—nothing more than a roof and walls—where the boat was housed.

They scurried to the boat, and Felipe released the moorings before shifting the vessel from the building and into the canal. Holding the ropes in one hand, he reached for her with the other, pulling her into his arm for a hug. "Can you come with me?"

"No," she said, looking up into his face, which bore a hopeful look. "You will travel better alone, as I must."

"You are traveling? Where will you go?"

"Back to the lands of my father, a land known anciently as *Zarahemla*." She tried to keep her tone light and wanted to hold back the tears which threatened to fall. Until this very moment, she hadn't realized how much she had grown to like and respect this stranger from a distant land, a land she could not comprehend. "I must return to my parents and seek for myself the answer to this mystery of the Great White God."

"Go in peace and safety," he said. "I too will return to the lands of my father."

"And to Manuela." A smile played against her lips as she hugged him.

"Yes," he said. "I will never forget you, my friend. Gracias."

Felipe had taught her so much about the world beyond the shores of Tenochtitlan, about other cultures and the people who came from lands beyond the tides across the seas. A swell of love rose within her breast, not only for Felipe, but also for Manuela, the girl he had left behind. Tia knew she would never forget him either.

She pulled away from their embrace, and Felipe stepped onto the boat. He took a seat at the aft and picked up a single paddle. "Which direction?" She pointed to the east, away from the already setting sun, and he began to row.

"Good-bye, Feli—pe." Her voice broke as she said his name, but her resolve was firm. "May God be with you."

"And with you." He waved, then turned again forward in his seat and kept a steady rhythm as he drew away from the palace toward the tree-lined distant shore and his next step home.

She stood watching him until the sun dropped behind the trees. Re-entering the palace, she knew she had a long night of preparation for her own journey before the sun arose.

41

Coins rattled inside the purse Manuela carried away from the docks. A sea captain, set to depart mid-day for Madrid, had purchased every embroidered piece she had shown him. His price had been more than fair, and she couldn't keep herself from smiling as she mentally added the new coins to those already in her chest at home. She wandered among the merchant stalls lining the street.

Eduardo found her moments after she left the docks. "Manuela, have you heard the news?" His voice was breathy as though he had run to catch up with her.

Her heart leaped and words refused to come at first. "News?" Could there be word about the ships' return? She had just been at the docks and seen only the activity of men preparing for departure. "Have you heard . . . ?"

"Yes," Eduardo said then reached out his hand to touch her arm.

Would her Felipe come home at last? She had so much to tell him. So much to share. Perhaps she should have visited César's mother yesterday to lift the betrothal. Now she would be forced to face César himself, but the determination within Manuela's heart to escape this unwanted engagement would not be moved. *Oh, Felipe. My love for you has grown a hundredfold.*

"His mother even now wails, crying that she knows her son is dead." Eduardo's smile seemed as though he were pleased.

Manuela heard him, but she couldn't make meaning at first. Then the words struck her heart as if an arrow had pierced her very soul. Suddenly feeling faint, she leaned into Eduardo for support. "What are you saying? That Felipe is . . . dead?"

"No, Manuela." Eduardo shook his head and helped her to a stone bench in the plaza then he squatted in front of her, rubbing her hands as he spoke in gentle, soothing tones. "You have not heard, and I, the fool, have made you fear the worst. It is César's mother, Señora Caballeria, of whom I speak. The ships have not returned to the docks, nor have they been sighted across the vast waters."

Tears continued to stream down her face, but she lifted her eyes to seek the truth from Eduardo.

He moved to sit beside her on the bench before speaking. "This morning, early, word passed through the village that César's mother had a vision. She dreamed that her son was killed . . . attacked from behind. A blow to his head with a weapon she could not identify. She swears it is true, and none of the village women have been able to calm her troubled soul."

Could such a dream be true? Manuela had heard of instances where mothers were given knowledge of an injury—

even forewarned of death—of a loved one. She had no reason to doubt the dreams of César's widowed mother, but perhaps the woman had merely succumbed to the fears that had also nagged Manuela about Felipe. Her own dreams had been confused—Felipe was home, yet on a ship that sailed away from the harbor. He had never left, yet he had never returned.

She began to think about what César's mother must have experienced in all the time her son was gone. Alone, and now dreaming her son was gone forever. Manuela's heart softened toward the woman with the grief she must feel. Thoughts of the loss of her own mother told her what she must do.

"Take me to her," she instructed Eduardo as she rose from her seat. "It is my place to calm her heart. Only I can do it. No other can unless her son came to her side."

"Are you certain?"

"Yes. I am bound by law to be her daughter. I should be the one to succor her in her grief."

The distance to César's home was not far. A dusty path led to the small adobe home. Several women Manuela recognized stood in the garden area. Eduardo stopped at the gate, and the women parted to let her pass. Their words were lost as fear pumped through her body. She had never met César's mother and did not know how to greet her. She felt inadequate, yet she knew that coming here was the right thing to do. The others seemed to acknowledge this as well. They reached to pat her arm and mumble soothing words to her as she passed.

When at last she reached the door, a woman she recognized from town—Doña Guadalupe Renteria—ushered her through the opening and spoke a single word directed toward the black-shawled woman seated within. "Manuela."

The older woman raised her head from the cupped palms of her hands. Her cheeks were reddened and puffy. Tears coursed down them. She held her arms open in a gesture of welcome. "My daughter," Señora Caballeria said, as she rose from her chair.

Despite having no social training from a mother, Manuela still understood what to do. She stepped toward the woman and allowed herself to be embraced by the loving arms of the mother of the young man she most hated. She was surprised by the woman's diminutive stature. The loose bun of silver-streaked hair at the nape of her neck gave her a gentle appearance. Her moist eyes bore kindness. Manuela felt a softening of her heart, as she thought of the final loving moments in her own mother's arms.

"I saw César running toward a great building, a strange, ornate palace." The woman's voice was so faint at first that Manuela had to strain to hear and understand what she was saying. "He had another lad with him, about his same age, also from Santiago de Cuba." She pulled away from Manuela and lifted the corner of her lace shawl to dab at the tears.

A stab sliced Manuela's heart. *Felipe.* Her knees began to buckle. She pulled in great gulps of air and hoped the pounding beats of her heart would stop so she could hear the words César's mother spoke. She recovered quickly as Señora Cabelleria continued.

"Before my son reached the gates, a weapon flew through the air, striking him in the back of the head and sending him to his death." She touched her hand against her heart and patted as though she wished to still the pattern of its beat. "A young woman reached for the other lad and pulled him within the walls of the gardens." As though retelling the story had drained every ounce of energy from her, the señora leaned against Manuela, allowing her to help her return to her seat.

She knelt before the señora then lifted the woman's wrinkled fingers into her palm. *What of the other lad and the young woman? Could the boy be Felipe?* Manuela had no way of knowing. Emotions bubbled within her in a mad dance which held her words silent. Although she sensed disquiet among those who stood nearby, Manuela simply did not know what to say. *Can an old woman's dream truly be accepted as prophesy?* If so, Manuela couldn't express sadness, for she didn't feel any. She dare not express her joy at being released of her betrothal through César's death. Her thoughts continued to center around the fate of her beloved Felipe.

At last, Eduardo stepped to her side. "It is time we go, Manuela." She was relieved that Eduardo had spoken for her. He kept his hand cupped around her elbow until she rose to her feet. "Until we hear from the expedition . . ."

"And when that happens," César's mother said, "I will see you again, at mass in memory of my son. May God bless you to overcome the grief his loss will bring you, dear girl."

42

Tia needed little time to collect her belongings. She tied the clothing into a parcel and fashioned a strap to carry them on her back, keeping her hands free. Although her fear at remaining within the palace walls was great, the thought of leaving the enclosure during the night held a different fear. Smoke from the temple sacrifices had covered the sky during the day. Still, the unnatural darkness clung to the moon, blocking all light. The odor of burning flesh permeated the air.

She knew her body required rest before the morning's journey, but she could not sleep. The memory of the attack against César repeated itself behind her eyelids each time she closed them. Would her fate be the same on the morrow?

"Tia?" Malinche slipped through the doorway and moved toward Tia's mat. "Are you sleeping?"

Tia sat up and motioned for her friend to join her. "No. My mind will not be still."

"I'm sorry." Malinche folded her legs beneath her as she took a place next to her friend upon the woven husks of maize. "Would it ease your mind to talk?"

"I think so." Tia rose and moved toward the remaining fire that glowed in the corner grate. Prodding a single ember from the pile, she placed a candlewick it against to produce a flame. "I keep seeing the last moment, when the Spaniard was killed."

"It is difficult to forget such violence," Malinche said, patting her hand against Tia's in a soothing gesture. "What will you now do?"

"It has been long since I've seen my mother," Tia said. "I wonder what she will think to learn her daughter has returned from the palace of the great emperor. Do you suppose word has reached the south of the events in Tenochtitlan?" She squatted by her mat, setting the candle in a firm position before rejoining Malinche.

"The massacres have been widespread. I do not see how this message would not have reached our homeland." Malinche dropped her head into her hands and a great sob racked through her body. "What have I done? How could I have betrayed my people so?"

At first Tia was uncertain about what her friend meant then she realized Malinche served Cortés in many ways, but she had also become his wife. "Malinche, you are not to blame."

She looked toward Tia, hope in her eyes. "I am his wife. Could I not have stopped him?"

"No one can stop a man when he has the fire of gold in his heart. Only he can pull away from such lustful desires." As she patted Malinche's hand, a sudden loneliness swept through her. How she would miss this woman who had taught her about the world beyond the palace walls. She would likely never see her again.

Malinche composed herself then asked, "What did you think your life would be like when you first came to Moctezuma's palace as a servant to Aramonia?"

Tia gave a deep sigh. "I thought that it would be exciting and wonderful. I lived the first twelve years of my life in the country, far away from the palace. We were farming people. Every day I helped my mother with the crops, but rarely did we produce more than what we needed." Tears sprang to her eyes, and a cough overtook her words for a moment. At last she again spoke. "How did my mother ever let me go?"

Malinche reached out to embrace her. "Of course, it is an honor to be a slave, and a slave for the emperor's chief wife is the greatest honor of all."

Returning the hug, she understood that Malinche's life was much the same as hers—the words her own.

"My mother cried when I was taken from her," Malinche said. "I cried, too, and I continue to cry, although now I have been gone two years from her side."

"I thought you had been gone longer." She was surprised that she had been away from her mother a year longer at three, yet she knew so much less than her friend about the world around her.

"Before my father died, I had many opportunities come to me," Malinche said. "Once he was gone, my new father did not want me . . . and here I am . . . a murderer's bride."

"No different in that respect than Aramonia," Tia said. "And perhaps the same is in store for me." Her voice took on a wistful tone as she continued, "I have just passed the anniversary of my fifteenth year of age. If I were at home, my parents might let me entertain some of the boys as a possible marriage partner. My body has developed and ripened, ready to bear children. But all choice was taken from me at the palace." *One more reason for me to leave now, while I can still escape. Or my life will be over—either married against my will or sacrificed to the gods in the temple.* She shook her head, trying to clear those thoughts away. "If I had to describe my feelings here at the palace, the word would be *lonely.*"

"A feeling I well understand." Malinche fingered the stitches in her night shawl. "But I fear the loneliness within me will only become greater. The day will come when I will no longer be among our people."

Thoughts raced across her mind. Did Malinche mean she was leaving? Did she fear her own death? Both possibilities were too real. "What are you saying?"

"The time comes when Cortés will return to the land he calls *Cuba,* and then on to Spain. As his mistress, I will go with him—*if* we both make it from this city alive." Malinche wiped a tear before patting her hand against her mouth, trying to beat back her growing yawn.

Tia wondered how the woman could she be so tired, yet so afraid at the same time? "You mustn't say these things. Of course you will survive." She said the words not only to assure Malinche, but also herself as she contemplated her plans. The first threads of dawn appeared through the window. *It's nearly time.* "Just think of the adventure of visiting a new land." *Would I want my journey to be an adventure?*

Malinche lay on her side as she fought off another yawn. "I'm too old for adventure. Cortés sees me as a great prize, a doll who speaks, one to impress those from his homeland. I will be a slave for the rest of my life." She closed her eyes.

"No one can hold you a slave within your heart," Tia said, but she knew her friend did not hear her. Malinche's deep breaths indicated she was sleeping. "Take care, my friend. Although we may never meet again, your friendship will always remain true in my heart. The man you now serve is not the White God, but I may know where to find him."

She rose from the mat and fastened her satchel in place by slipping her arms though the straps. With a final glance toward Malinche, Tia turned and stole across the room, then passed through the garden door.

The rays of first sun peeked above the trees as she hurried across the cobblestones and into the streets on her way toward her mother, and home.

43

The journey to the seashore was much easier and quicker than Felipe expected. He had not realized how the initial foray into the city he knew as Tenochtitlan wandered south before Cortés brought them toward the island and Moctezuma. His plan was to travel as true toward the rising sun as possible, then search the coastline until he located the second set of ships that Velasquez had sent. Surely these men would not deny him passage to return to his homeland.

The morning sun struck the water in a sparkling array like a field of gems. The anchored ship was shrouded at its base by a skirt of fog. It seemed to Felipe that its presence, a mere dream. He had expected to spend at least a day traveling north, then south in search of the ship.

A handful of men dotted the sandy beach, moving from their rowboats to the camp where they warmed themselves at the scattered fires. Their steel breastplates and helmets assured him they were part of the Spanish delegation.

Now was no more time for hesitation. "Ahoy," Felipe called as he strode toward the men. "Ahoy."

It seemed each man stopped to see who called out to

them. Some drew weapons, others stood as though their bones had locked. "Halt!" one man shouted.

Felipe obeyed the order. He dropped to his knees and called, "Amigo. I am Felipe de Santiago de Cuba. I have left the company of Hérnan Cortés in search of safe passage back to my homeland. I have no money to pay you, nothing but my gratitude and service to give if you but grant my wish and take me to the land of my father."

Chattering erupted almost immediately among the men, and several rushed forward to greet Felipe. "Of course, my son," a tall, dark-bearded man said. He reached an arm to help Felipe from his kneeling position. "You are our brother, and we will be pleased to have you join our company."

The sense of relief washed through Felipe. Tears sprang to his eyes as he grabbed the man in a strong hug. "*Gracias. Gracias.*"

The man guided Felipe toward the camp where another man offered him food and fresh water to drink. The ordeal was over. At last, he would return home to his sweet Manuela.

Her trip home did not take as long as Tia expected. Her longer legs as a young woman carried her more swiftly that they had three years before when she was but a girl. She believed that the desire in her heart to escape the palace, escape the horror of living under the roof of Moctezuma had added to the speed with which she had made her journey.

The place seemed just the same as always. Her home

was small, but inviting. Flowers decorated the entrance into the vegetable garden, and evidence that her mother had been doing the washing met her at the back gate. Her father's tools sat upon a bench outside the entrance to their home.

My home, she thought, a wide smile almost hurting her face. She stood for only a moment longer, breathing in the fresh air, untainted by the smoke and stench of burning flesh. A prayer of thanks burned deep in her heart. At last she was home.

Home to her mother. The home of her father.

And the home where at last she could find out the truth about the great White God, the God her parents had embraced.

44

A pounding at the door woke Manuela from a deep sleep. She rolled out of bed, wrapping a shawl around her shoulders, and shuffled toward the door. *Who can this be before the sun has even risen in the sky?* She glanced toward her papa's cot but saw that he had already left for the morning, out to tend his cattle before the rising August heat. She found Eduardo leaning against the door jam, bent over double as he struggled for breath. Again he had been running.

This time she allowed herself no fear, only useless hope. "What is it?" she said, wishing her friend had brought the news she had waited for so long. "The ships? Are they returned at last?"

When Eduardo shook his head *no*, Manuela could feel hope rush from her mind and heart like water through an opened canal. "Come in and sit. I will get you a drink." She reached toward him, but Eduardo waved his hand to again say *no*.

"The ships . . . at the dock . . ." He tried to compose himself, gasping for breath. "Velasquez has returned . . . he has brought men from the expedition . . . Felipe . . . Felipe . . ."

Manuela's heart surged against her chest, beating rapid and powerful like the tides of the sea washing over her. She grabbed Eduardo's arm. "Have you seen him?"

He was taking more regular and deep breaths than a moment ago. "I saw him standing at the top rail and called out to him. He waved back. I ran as fast as I could to tell you. If we hurry, he will still be there. Velasquez will not release the men before the treasures are unloaded."

"It will only take me a moment to dress," she said as she moved toward the drawn curtain around her bed. She couldn't move fast enough. The wait was over. Felipe was home at last. So many days she had spent at the wharf, and she wanted to be there again, now that he had returned.

What if she did not recognize him? How will he have changed? Tugging her dressing gown over her head then tossing it aside, she slipped her feet into leather sandals and wiggled petticoats over her head. Next a brightly colored skirt settled at her waistline. A fresh white blouse completed her outfit. She ran her fingers through her hair and lifted it away from the nape of her neck, tying it with a ribbon as she stepped from behind the curtain.

"I am ready," she said.

Eduardo rose from his seat. "Felipe is a lucky man," he said as he looked at her.

A blush warmed her cheeks, but she kept her mind on the ships and Felipe. "We must hurry."

Manuela had made her way to the docks so many times that she did not even think about which way to go as she ran from one street to the next. Her village had grown in the past two years. The number of people living within Santiago's borders caused the narrow streets to feel crowded. But at this hour, only a few early fisherman and merchants were preparing their wares on the cobblestone as Manuela and Eduardo passed toward the ships.

"Did he look well?" Manuela asked. "Has he changed?"

"I only saw him from a distance." Eduardo waved his hand in a gesture indicating *no* to the fish monger. The merchant tried to keep up with their hurrying steps but left them in less than the distance of a city square.

The smell of salty ocean breeze sent waves of excitement through Manuela. She started running faster. Soon she could see the ships. Guidelines from the upper decks were tied to the docks. Crates had been moved onto the wharf, and men were in the process of disembarking. Many had cotton bags hung over their shoulders, which likely held their clothing. Felipe would have had none of these things as his journey began, Manuela realized. How had he fared in the time he had been gone?

It seemed hundreds of people lined the shoreline, like the day Cortés posted his call to service and asked for men to join him. Manuela worked her way through the crowd, looking at everyone in hopes of finding Felipe. She spotted Papa also making his way toward the docks, but she only cared to see Felipe. Never had she missed him more now that she knew he was so near.

Once she found herself caught in the middle of a family who had stopped to select fruits for their daily meals.

"*Perdón, perdón,*" Manuela said, but the children

swarmed around her feet, almost tripping her. Their squealing laughter told her she had become a part of their game, but she didn't have time for childish play. Felipe might have already left the docks. After all this time, she needed to be at the wharf to make all those hours spent, staring off into the distance beyond the shipyards complete.

"Manuela, over here." Eduardo's arm snaked past the children and tugged her toward him. "I think I see him." Another step and she was free from the children.

"*Lo siento,*" their mother said as she gathered them closer to her skirts, away from Manuela.

Eduardo placed a hand at the small of her back to guide her. "He was hanging over the railing on the first ship. It looked like he was searching the people standing below. Most likely for you." They moved through the crowd which had gathered, side-stepping to avoid anyone who stood in their way.

"Manuela!"

She heard the shout and, despite the deeper resonance, recognized Felipe's voice. Her heart stopped then pounded harder than she had ever known before. *Felipe!* She scanned the men. Worn clothes, scruffy beards, matted hair—the sailors all looked the same. *How will I ever know him?* And then, she saw him. There was no doubt. His walk was the same as always. His dark hair was longer, and his face looked tired, but he was the same boy she loved only now he looked like a man.

He wended through others moving toward the ship's gangplank. Manuela took a few steps more then waited, not wanting him to lose her in the mass of people gathering to greet others from the returning ships. Eduardo stood impatiently next to her, also trying to view Felipe's progress above the heads of the crowd. Time passed too slowly.

"Why is he taking so long to get here?" Manuela asked, glaring at Eduardo as though it was him who had caused the delay.

Before he could respond, Felipe called, "Manuela, Eduardo, over here!"

The crowd parted, and at last she saw him. He stood talking with her papa as she and Eduardo converged upon them.

"Welcome home." The two friends embraced then Eduardo gave Felipe a hearty slap on the shoulder.

"Welcome home, indeed," Felipe said as he stepped forward to embrace Manuela. "And there is no place else I would rather be."

"My son," her papa said as he clasped Felipe's hand. "You have proven yourself far beyond what I ever thought possible." As though he could see Felipe preparing to protest, he held his other hand up to stop him. "Gold does not a man make. Honesty, integrity, and loyalty, a willingness to carry through with his obligations, and a deep abiding love for his fellow man . . . and woman. These are all traits I have always known to be within you. I am sorry I did not acknowledge them before your journey." He glanced toward Manuela, a twinkle in his eye. "These are the things that make a man great. I would be pleased to see my daughter wed to you."

An overwhelming desire to hug her papa brought Manuela to him before Felipe could respond. Giving a little jump, she wrapped her arms around his broad shoulders and hung there like she had as a young child. "Oh, Papa. Thank you. Thank you. You have made me so happy."

A hearty laugh escaped from deep within his chest as he held her close then twirled her around and around, ignoring the people around them. "Now the joy is returned in my sweet daughter." He stopped and set her feet on the ground, holding her at arm's length and looking her over as if seeing her for the first time. "And she has become a woman." He planted a kiss on her cheek before placing her left hand in Felipe's. "And you are a man worthy of a bride such as she. My blessings to you both."

"Thank you, sir," Felipe said as he again shook the man's hand. "I will not let you down."

"I know," her papa said. "I will leave the two of you to your planning. I must be off to prepare the fatted calf. Come Eduardo. We will soon have a celebration that will be the envy of all of Cuba."

As the two of them left, Manuela's gaze turned toward the man who would become her husband. The warmth in Felipe's eyes confirmed the feelings in her heart. The time spent apart had only drawn them closer together.

"Manuela, I was a fool. My new world was here in Cuba all along; here with you."

He ran the tip of his finger over her lips. A tingle coursed through her body. Manuela stepped closer into his arms. "You were a child, my sweet Felipe. And now you *are* a man. The man I love has returned to me."

"And our home will be all the world I will ever need."

He kissed her with all the tenderness and love Manuela would ever need.

Acknowledgments

Readers often ask, "Where did you come up with the idea for this story?"

Tides Across the Sea did not begin as a Young Adult historical, nor was it a romance. The original idea came from my husband shortly after we were married, and the book was supposed to be an adult thriller set in southern Utah, where a group of men were searching through caves in hope of finding Moctezuma's hidden treasures of gold.

But I hang out with junior high school kids all day. What did I know about writing an adult thriller from a male point of view, especially since I spend most of my time reading young adult novels? After several false starts, Manuela and Felipe were born, and the thriller idea had died like some of the explorers seeking after those caves had apparently done.

One of the fun things about being an English teacher and a writer is that I had a build-in audience to test market my book, and I'd trained young editors well enough that many of these students knew how to deliver a sharp critique, which made me stretch as a writer. Thanks to M. Belen

Monyano and Angie Newman Day, who is now an author herself, for not being afraid to tell their teacher when she got something wrong. I'd also like to thank Brandon Peterson for his incredible job of acting out every scene when I read the book aloud to my 7th grade Honors English class a few years ago. The moment of "Land Ho" was a classic!

As always, the members of my critique group have been my most supportive fans. From the early years with Stephanni Hicken Meyers, the late Sandy Hirche, Sherry Schloss, and Lynda Keith, to the current version of Annette Lyon, Michele Paige Holmes, Heather B. Moore, J. Scott Savage, Sarah M. Eden, and Robison Wells, I've learned so much from all of you. Thanks for always being there.

I'd like to add a special Thank You to Jaimey Grant, my cover designer. She has brought me absolutely gorgeous covers for not only this novel, but also for *A Note Worth Taking* and *Leona & Me, Helen Marie.* I'm totally in love with every one of them and so thankful I found her. Her enthusiasm has been unparalleled and I couldn't ask for someone nicer than she is to work with.

But the biggest thanks of all belongs to my husband, Mike, who not only told me tales of Moctezuma's gold, but who also allows me the time I need to write and revise, who listens to the response from a query whether positive or negative, and who wants to fight my literary battles for me, even though we know they are something I must face alone. You are "all the tenderness and love *I* would ever need."

About the Author

Lu Ann Brobst Staheli got her start as a celebrity paparazzi-stalker-chick, which led to her award-winning career as a ghostwriter for celebrity memoirs. A masochist at heart, she taught junior high school English for 33 years, moved to the school library beginning year 34, and once spent two weeks summer vacation backpacking through Europe with fifteen of her students. She has won three Best of State Medals—two for writing and one for teaching—but refuses to wear them all at the same time because she'd hate to be known as a show-off. Her other published works include *The Explorers: Tides Across the Sea*; *Leona & Me, Helen Marie*; *A Note With Taking*; *When Hearts Conjoin*, the story of the conjoined Herrin twins; *Psychic Madman* about mentalist Jim Karol; *One Day at a Time: Teaching Secondary Language Arts*; and *Books, Books, and More Books: A Parent and Teacher's Guide to Adolescent Literature*. Lu Ann says, "But 2013 will be the year of the eBook for me. A long list of titles are in the finalization stage, and I'm excited to make them available to my readers."

Lu Ann's articles have appeared in Grit, Byline, Scouting, Library Media Connections, and The Writer magazines, and she is featured in the upcoming book release, *Best of The Writer*. She has published invitational essays in *Teaching Secondary Language Arts K-12: It Really Works* (Christopher-Gordon Publishers) and *Famous Family Nights* (Cedar Fort International).

As a Senior Editor with Precision Editing Group, Lu Ann Staheli has had a hand in a number of releases from Deseret Book, Shadow Mountain, Covenant Communications, and other regional publishers, including several winners and finalists for the Whitney Award and New York Times bestsellers. A former Associate Producer of Alan Osmond's Stadium of Fire, Lu Ann resides in Spanish Fork, Utah, with her husband, and tries to keep track of their five sons.

Praise for Lu Ann's Work

A Note Worth Taking

"This story should be a must-read for every middle grade/junior high girl. The hurt that Laura, the main character, suffers at the hand of Vickie, her supposed best friend, is one that so many girls this age will relate to. How Laura handles the school situation and her pain, along with the growth she experiences throughout the story, are what make this book stand out. Good lessons and good times. Adults reading the story will enjoy the nostalgia of days gone by~as well as being grateful those days are past. We all survived junior high! Laura does too, and you'll cheer for her triumphs over mean girls and her blossoming maturity and self-worth."

—Michele Paige Holmes, Whitney Award-winning author

Leona & Me, Helen Marie

"A delightful middle grade novel from award-winning author, Lu Ann Staheli. Readers will fall in love with Helen Marie, a precocious seven-year-old, who looks up to her older sister, Leona Mae, the two of them getting into trouble more often or not (think Laura Ingalls . . .). I laughed out loud at

Helen Marie's antics and loved her relationship with her mother and father. Set in 1922 southern Indiana, the family faces financial hardships, like so many around them. But they are blessed with a humble life, rich with country living, and take pride in hard work."

—H. B. Moore, Utah Best of State and Whitney Award-winning author

Tides Across the Sea

"A good read for the 12–16 age range and is a beautiful coming of age and young love story. The author obviously did an extensive amount of research and it shows in the scenery, language and tone of the book. There is plenty of action, following not only the main couple, but also a young slave girl in the palace of Montezuma. Both sides continue to build until the truth of Cortez's expedition comes to a head . . . *Tides Across the Sea* sends young readers deep into history and gives them a story they will find difficult to put down!"

—Stephenia McGee, InD'Tale Magazine

www.ingramcontent.com/pod-product-compliance
Lightning Source LLC
Chambersburg PA
CBHW051948220626
47052CB00004B/849